THE OLD AND THE LOST

Johns Hopkins: Poetry and Fiction
John T. Irwin, General Editor

THE OLD AND THE LOST

Collected Stories
BY GLENN BLAKE

Johns Hopkins University Press
Baltimore

This book has been brought to publication with the generous assistance of the Poetry and Fiction Fund.

Johns Hopkins University Press
2715 North Charles Street
Baltimore, Maryland 21218-4363
www.press.jhu.edu

Library of Congress Cataloging-in-Publication Data

Names: Blake, Glenn.
Title: The Old and the Lost : collected stories / by Glenn Blake.
Description: Baltimore, Maryland : Johns Hopkins University Press, 2016. |
Series: Johns Hopkins: poetry and fiction
Identifiers: LCCN 2016007279| ISBN 9781421421032 (pbk. : alk. paper) | ISBN 9781421421049 (electronic) | ISBN 1421421038 (pbk. : alk. paper) | ISBN 1421421046 (electronic)
Subjects: LCSH: Texas, South—Fiction. | Southern States—Social life and customs—Fiction.
Classification: LCC PS3552.L34825 A6 2016 | DDC 813/.54—dc23
LC record available at https://lccn.loc.gov/2016007279

A catalog record for this book is available from the British Library.

Special discounts are available for bulk purchases of this book. For more information, please contact Special Sales at 410-516-6936 or specialsales@press.jhu.edu.

Johns Hopkins University Press uses environmentally friendly book materials, including recycled text paper that is composed of at least 30 percent post-consumer waste, whenever possible.

John T. Irwin

In Memory of George Manner

CONTENTS

THE OLD AND THE LOST

RETURN FIRE

For John McNamara

HE'S SITTING on the verandah, underneath the magnolias. The sun's going down. His backyard's in shadow. The sun's shining on the bayou and on the levee bluff beyond the bayou.

He's sitting out there, sipping his mescal. None of this hokey Hollywood horseshit. None of this knocking back shots, chugging the bottle, worrying the worm. This isn't pulque. This isn't tequila. He likes to keep the bottle in the freezer so that when he pours the maguey, it's viscous—not quite liquid, not quite solid. He likes the smoky taste. He likes to watch the mescal move. It doesn't just sit there like bourbon. It doesn't bubble like champagne. It doesn't foam like beer. It slowly, practically imperceptibly, roils in the glass. It's like watching a tannic pond, its bottom lined with leaves—days, weeks, months—turn itself over.

Angela loved the magnolias. She loved to sit out there. She loved to open the windows in the springtime and let the breeze from the bayou fill the house with that sweet Southern smell. She loved to pick a blossom and float it in a bowl and place the bowl between them during dinner. But they died so quickly, those magnolia blossoms, overnight, so in the mornings, before he shaved, before he fixed breakfast, he scooped them out and tossed them over the verandah.

He's thinking these things when he notices a hummingbird hovering over his drink. He's thinking, Ruby throat. He's thinking, Female. No blood-red bandana. The hummingbird alights on the lip of his glass. She's considering the contents of his container. She starts to tongue the nectar.

I wouldn't, he says, and she disappears.

He pours himself some more mescal. No ice. One quarter lime. He watches the worm writhe in the bottle.

He notices the hummingbird feeder hanging in the magnolia. He positioned it so that she could see it from the kitchen window. The feeder's empty. The feeder's been empty these many months. He's thinking, Four shots water, one shot sugar. He's thinking, Four shots sugar, one shot water. Something gets boiled. He could probably fill it.

He's thinking these things when he notices the ruby throat visiting the magnolia. She visits each of the feeder's ports, and then she darts back over and stops right in front of him. She's just hovering inches from his nose. The whirring's so loud, so close. This isn't mescaline, this isn't peyote, but he can see perfectly—in slow motion—the figure-eight patterns of her wings. She's just suspended there. She's just watching him. He can see her blink. Sorry, he says, and the hummingbird feeder, hanging in the magnolia, explodes.

He hears the laughter from across the bayou. He doesn't need to look. It's the Bagwells. On the other side of the water. In the next county. What are they now? Juniors? Seniors? Varsity football. Twins. He knows that. Over at James Bowie. Old man Buddy's boys.

HE DROVE over once to talk to the old man. There used to be a ferry on Ferry Road. You'd drive your truck onto the floating

barge, unhook the chain, and then pull yourself across. But Carla
had taken care of the landing, and the ferry had never been found.
So now you had to follow the bayou down through the slough to
the interstate. Sometimes an hour depending on the tides. You
had to cross over the Old and the Lost, drive past rice field after
rice field, down farm-to-market roads, until you reached the cattle
guard. The gate was always locked, so you had to climb over and
try to make the mile back to the big house, back in the live oaks,
before the big dogs found you and took you down. But his old man
and old man Buddy had never gotten along, so he said, Fuck it,
before he made it through the slough, pulled off the road, and
turned around. He wondered what this country was like before
there were ferries, before there were bridges. Bayous and swamps.
Rivers and sloughs. No way in. No way out. Who in his right mind
would've settled here?

THEY STARTED out in junior high, climbing the bluff with their
.22, shooting at things in the bayou. Snakes and turtles. Working
their way up the food chain. Birds and squirrels. He finds rabbits
and armadillos when he mows along the shore.

He hears the rifle. He hears their laughter. He looks across the
water, and there they are, standing up on the bluff, wearing their
black letter jackets. The kicker's resting the rifle on his shoulder.
The quarterback's sporting bleached-blond hair. He's seen their
pictures in the newspaper.

They're just shooting, he says. They ain't aiming.

The quarterback's bent over with his hands on his knees. He's
laughing so hard he can't stand up.

He hears someone screaming, someone screaming next door.
Gladys? He's just sitting there, watching the Bagwells. They're
giving each other high-fives. They're just standing there, right

out in the open. The sun's going down behind him, and what's left's shining across the bayou, up the bluff, and into their eyes.

What's wrong with you, he says, shooting into the sun!

THOSE TWO sure terrorized Angela. She had a doe back then that came by in the evenings and grazed in the bottom close to the bayou. And before long there was a fawn, too, feeding down there with her mama. Angela sprinkled some corn for them, and he stood a salt block on a stump, and in the evenings they sat out there on the verandah and watched the doe and her fawn graze their way to the water until the sun went down, and the dark came up, and all they could see of the two deer were the bright white spots on the back of the fawn.

He remembers the afternoon when he came home from work, and her car was in the driveway. He opened the front door and said, Knock, knock and walked into the den and placed his lunch box on the bar. He remembers the back door was open, and when he looked down their yard to the water, there she was, her back to him, kneeling by the bayou. He remembers shouting her name, running down the yard, kneeling there beside her, and when she turned to look at him, she was cradling the fawn and crying.

HE'S THINKING these things as he lifts his glass, and as he lifts his glass, the bottle of mescal explodes.

He's just sitting out there, staring at what's left of the bottle. The neck gone. The top half missing. He hears someone screaming, and in between the screams, he hears the laughter.

He finishes his drink. He pushes his chair away from the table. He stands, opens the screen door, and walks inside. It's dark in there, so he can see the hole in the screen where the slug tore through. He looks across the room at the cabinet and sees the shattered china.

He walks downstairs into the bedroom and opens the closet. He pushes the hangers of work clothes to the right and finds the side-by-sides, the over-and-unders, the semiautomatics, the pumps. The .410. The 20 gauge. The 16 gauge. The 12. He pushes the hangers to the left and finds the leather cases. The lever actions. The bolt actions. The .243. The .270. The .30-30. The .30-06. The Weatherby .300 magnum. He reaches in and removes the case.

He climbs the stairs and notices the stack of newspapers. He grabs one, and while he's at it, he grabs a cushion from the love seat. He walks into the kitchen and opens the pantry. He feels around in there until he finds the package with the cheesecloth. He leaves the dark kitchen, opens the screen door, and walks onto the verandah.

He tosses the newspaper into the empty chair. He drops the cushion onto the table. He rests the rifle case upon the cushion. He drapes the cheesecloth over what's left of the bottle. He moves his chair so that it faces the far shore.

The shadows have blanketed the bayou, have climbed the bluff to their feet. They couldn't see him now if they tried. The kicker hands the rifle to his brother. He points at something across the water. He shields his eyes against the sun.

He positions the cushion on the table. He unzips the case and removes the Weatherby. He removes the caps from the scope. He rests the rifle upon the cushion. He sits down.

He hears something pass through the tops of the magnolias, the riflefire, the dry, leathery leaves pattering down around him. He hears the kicker whistling. He sees him waving across the water.

I see you, he says. Don't you worry. He slams a shell into the chamber. He turns his baseball cap around. He looks through the scope until he finds them. He selects the kicker. He drags the crosshairs from head to toe. Skull, sternum, navel, groin. He's thinking, .300 magnum. He's thinking, Two hundred yards. He's thinking, Kneecap.

The quarterback's reloading. They're looking down the bayou, their backs to him. They're digging in the pockets of their jackets. The kicker's hooting and hollering.

Turn around, he says. His finger finds the trigger.

They're wrestling for the rifle. The kicker snatches it away.

Fine, he says. He's thinking, Left leg. He's thinking, Right leg. He's thinking, Back of the knee. And before he fires, he says, What you boys know about shooting?

He watches the boy's leg kick the ball through the uprights, lift him high into the sky, up over his head, flip him perfectly, and then drop him down on his back.

No more field goals for you, he says. No more extra points.

He hears someone screaming, except this time it's coming from across the water. The quarterback falls to his knees. He grabs his brother's jacket and drags him down the other side of the levee.

He slams another shell into the chamber. He scans the bluff to the north. He scans the bluff to the south. He's looking for a blond head, a black torso, a rifle pointed in his direction.

He hears someone screaming. He hears someone shouting.

He rests the rifle upon the cushion. He grabs what's left of the bottle. He fishes around in the bottom for the largest shards of glass. He feels around in there with his fingers.

He drapes the cheesecloth over the jagged edge. He grabs the newspaper and removes the rubber band. He doubles the rubber band and then stretches it over the cheesecloth. He tugs at the corners of the cloth so that the fit's snug, the surface taut. He pours himself another drink.

The sun's gone down. The shadowline's made the Sabine by now. Louisiana maybe. Mississippi soon. Everything in the evening becomes the same black. The barn. The yard. The trees. If someone were standing down there by the water, he wouldn't be able to see them. The bayou's shining like liquid mercury, reflecting perfectly the same smooth silver of the sky.

The scope's almost useless now. He scans the still surface to the north and to the south for some disturbance, for some ripple, for someone wading across to flank him.

He's sitting out there on the verandah. The bottle's empty. The rifle's propped against the door. He hears the cicadas on every branch, in every tree, and if he listens carefully, he can hear the crickets beneath the cicadas. He hears someone sobbing through the darkness.

He's sitting out there, watching the fireflies drift across the water. The night's thick with them. He tries to follow the fireflies between flashes. Here—one thousand one, one thousand two—there. He sees things sometimes. The barbecue. The birdbath. The barn. The bottom's filled with a bright green fog.

He notices a pair of headlights shining on the levee. He sees these lights before he hears the tires on the oyster shells. A vehicle. A visitor. Over next door. At Gladys's. He watches the headlights dance down the levee as the vehicle follows the bend in the driveway.

He hears the engine stop, a door open, the wailing now. He hears a man's voice, a consoling voice. He can't hear what it's saying, but he can hear the tone, and he can just imagine. Hush, now. Settle down, now. Everything's gonna be all right.

He watches a spotlight scour the levee, climb the steep embankment, and then stop. He sees something on the other side of the water, a magnificent buck, glaring across the bayou, standing up there at the top of the bluff.

Everything's dark again. The backyard. The barn. The bottom. The night has a way of healing itself. He hears the bullfrogs from down around the bayou. He hears the man's voice—questions now—rising at the end of every line. He hears a car door close, the engine start, the patrol car ease along the fence line.

He's listening for the tires on the cattle guard, the tires on the highway. He's listening for the tires on his oyster-shell driveway. No headlights this time. No bright spotlight. No flashing red lights. Someone's coming. Someone's passed the gate. Someone's coasting across the lawn.

He's thinking, I'm next. My turn. He's thinking of the rifle propped against the door. One shell in the chamber. He's thinking, When was the last time we had company?

He watches the patrol car pass through the carport. He watches the deputy park behind the house. He's thinking, He killed the motor. He's thinking, He coasted back here. He looks down from the verandah and sees a face in the window, an elbow resting on the frame.

He hears the cicadas, the crickets, the ticking of the engine cooling. He hears someone clear his throat and then, Bobby Dean?

Austin, he says.

Nice night, Austin says.

Quiet, he says.

Quiet *now*, Austin says.

He hears Gladys shouting in the distance, Come on in, babies! Come on in!

How you been? Austin says.

I been fine, he says.

I wonder, Austin says. I wonder.

He hears Gladys singing through the darkness, Nighty night. Sleep tight.

We're all worried, Austin says. We're all worried about you.

I don't doubt it, he says.

He sees the lights go out next door. The corral. The barn. The pen. The porch. He sees the bedroom light come on, shining every night from the back of the house, shining through the same pink drapes since he was a boy.

Somebody bagged one of the Bagwell boys, Austin says.

Imagine that, he says.

The special teams player, Austin says. The kicker. Shot him in the leg. The right leg. Blew it right out from underneath him.

It's a mean world, he says.

Right over there, Austin says. Across the bayou. On that bluff. You been out here long?

Tonight, he says. The afternoon. Most of the day.

You hear anything? Austin says.

Some shots, he says. Those boys. Some gunfire. No more so than any other day.

Shot one of Gladys's kids, Austin says. Killed one of Gladys's kids.

No shit? he says.

One of her goats, Austin says. Killed one of her goats.

That Gladys loves her goats, he says.

We're thinking, .22, Austin says. We're thinking, .22 Long Rifle. What do you think?

.22, he says.

You hear anything else? Austin says. Any heavy artillery? We're thinking, Someone with a big rifle. Someone with a big gun.

A big gun, he says.

You still got that .300 Mag? Austin says. You save that Weatherby?

That Weatherby saved me, he says.

That boy, Austin says. I wonder if he'll walk.

He won't come limping back out to that bluff, he says.

I wouldn't think, Austin says.

So much for scholarships, he says.

I guess it was time, Austin says.

It was *past* time, he says.

He sees the bedroom light go out next door. Goodnight, Gladys, he says. Everything's dark now. Even the fireflies have gone to bed. Lloyd and Maxine, he says. How are they?

Fine, Austin says. Just fine. They're always asking about you.

Appreciate it, he says.

Daddy comes by every now and then and picks up your papers, Austin says, but he says nobody ever answers the door.

I'm probably out back, he says.

That's what he figured, Austin says. He figured you were.

Maybe next time, he says.

Listen, Austin says, why don't you come out to the house? Why don't you come out Sunday?

Not just yet, he says.

Mama and Daddy, Austin says, they'd love to see you. They *need* to see you.

Not just yet, he says.

It might help, Austin says. It just might.

I don't doubt it, he says.

In the distance, across the bayou, he hears the call of the barred owl, Who cooks for you? Who cooks for you all? He hears Angela's tambour on the mantel chime the late hour. He hears the radio static from the patrol car.

Sjolander, he says. You think Sjolander'll drive over?

He'll drive out to the big house, Austin says. The Bagwell place. He'll drive up to the cattle guard, but old man Buddy won't let him in. He'll drive up to the big bridge, to the Old and the Lost, but then he'll turn around and head back home.

The last of his kind, he says.

The only sheriff in Texas, Austin says, that won't cross a river.

But old man Buddy, he says. Old man Buddy'll cross a river.

He's got his hands full, Austin says. Drove that boy into Beaumont.

Yettie Kersting, he says.

Yettie Kersting, Austin says.

I can take care of myself, he says.

Austin shines the spotlight down the oyster shell to the highway. I wouldn't let just anybody drive up this driveway, he says. Don't you got a gate?

A gate won't stop them, he says.

You know, Austin says. He shines the spotlight down the yard, across the bayou, up the bluff. I promised Sister I'd look out for you.

You have, he says.

I gave her my word, Austin says.

You can't save me, he says.

Austin kills the spotlight. Fuck it, he says. It's over. It's done. Ain't nobody crying about that boy.

Everything has a way of working itself out, he says.

Listen to me, Bobby Dean, Austin says. He starts the engine. You take care of yourself, he says. He shifts into gear. You keep your eyes open.

Tell your mama and daddy I said hey, he says.

I'll do that, Austin says and drives away.

He's sitting out there on the verandah. He's listening to the tires on the oyster-shell driveway. He's watching the taillights disappear in the distance.

The sounds of the night return. The cicadas. The crickets. The bullfrogs from down around the bayou.

He hears the patrol car cross the cattle guard. He hears the creak of the gate. He hears the clatter of the chain.

Listen to me, Austin, he says. In this life, we don't always get what we want. We don't always get what we need. In this life, we get what we deserve.

DEGÜELLO

"Six until midnight," he says as we pass.

"Drive on," I say.

"Drive on?" he says. "Into the Channel? Where are we going?"

"1836," I say. "Here," I say. "Take a right up here."

He turns off the highway onto 1836, the road lined with live oaks. The magnificent monument, the shellstone star, shines bright white. He stops the cab outside the main entrance.

"Eight until eight," he says.

"Drive on," I say.

"It's two in the morning!" he says. "It's *past* two in the morning!" He hasn't turned around. Even in the dark, I can see his eyes in the mirror. "What about the rangers?" he says. "The... patrols?"

"Midnight and dawn," I say. "Drive on."

"Where are we going!" he says.

"We're close," I say.

[13]

"'To what!" he says. "Massacred Mexicans!'"

" 'There the bodies lay,' " I say, " 'turning to skeletons which grazing cattle chewed for their salt.' "

"Do you hear me?" he says. He turns in his seat. "One mile!" he says. "My ass is taking you in for one mile!"

"'Take a right," I say. "Take a right on the road to New Washington."

"New Washington?" he says. He takes a right. "I grew up around here. I grew up in this part of the country, and I ain't ever *heard* of New Washington! You sure you're in the right state?"

"It's a town," I say. "It *was* a town. Some two hundred years ago. I don't know. Maybe it slid off into the bay."

"I'll tell you where this road goes now," he says. "No town. No place. Nofuckingwhere."

I roll down the window and take a deep breath, and for the first time I smell the sloughs, the bayous, the rivers, the bays. "The Gulf of Mexico," I say.

I look off across the dark prairie to the marsh in the distance. "Mirabeau Buonaparte Lamar," I say. "This is almost the exact route of his cavalry as he cut off the Mexican retreat."

"Is that right?" he says. "Listen," he says, "why don't you let me take you back into Houston?" He turns around and looks at me. "Why don't you let me take you back into . . . *Shit!*" He slams on his brakes, and my head slams into the window frame.

"What!" I say, rubbing my head. "What is it!"

"The end of the line," he says, and then I see it. I see the road disappears under the water. The road disappears under the bay.

I open the door and step out of the cab. "Hit your brights," I say.

"What?" he says.

"Your bright lights," I say. "Your high beams."

Degüello

The entire battleground is underwater. The complete battlefield submerged, from the Mexican breastworks, from Santa Anna's camp, all the way to the bay.

The road becomes a turnaround, an oyster-shell loop around a granite marker. He follows it with his cab, the back door open.

Some half a mile across, I can see where the road climbs out of the water, up toward the ridgeline, back toward the bayou.

"Hop in," he says, pulling up beside me. He has his window down. He has his elbow out.

"Is it high tide?" I say.

"Do I look like a sailor?" he says.

"I mean, I wonder how *deep* it is."

"No way!" he says. "No fucking way! It's company policy: 'Under no circumstances—under no circumstances at all—are you to ever even consider driving your taxicab *underwater*!'"

"How much?"

"What?" he says.

"How much do I owe you?"

"Hop in," he says. *"Let's get the fuck out of here."*

"How much?" I say, untying my shoes.

"I ain't leaving you out here!" he says. "No phone. No one for . . . ten miles. Fifteen miles. No one *living*! There's nothing out here!"

I take off my shoes. "You don't see it, do you?"

"See what?" he says.

I take off my socks.

"You're swimming across, are you?"

"Wading across," I say. "It can't be *that* deep."

"Come on and pay me then," he says. "Come on and pay me before you go and drown yourself."

I pay him the fare. "It's only death," I say.

He laughs. "That's right," he says. "That's *all* it is," he says. He shifts the cab into drive. "And it's waiting for your ass at the bottom of the bay."

I rest a foot on the granite marker. I roll up a pants leg. I can see the red taillights following the road back to the entrance, back to the highway, back to Houston. I roll up the other pants leg. The cab gone now.

I look across the water to the far shore. There are no lights. There are only long, low silhouettes of live oaks mirrored in the bay. A southeast breeze coming in from the Gulf. A gull? A tern?

"WHERE'S YOUR car!" I hear him before I see him. I'm walking down Battleground Road, my pants wet, my shoes in my hand, when he hits me with his spotlight and shouts, "Where's your car!"

"In Baltimore!" I shout back, shielding my eyes.

"You walked in from Baltimore, did you?" I can see him now, standing up in the tower, at the top of the ladder, in the door of the wheelhouse.

"I *flew* in," I say. "I *flew* into Hobby." I stop at the landing. The chain is up. Painted on each side of the tower is the word, "Lynch."

"That's quite a hike in itself," he says. "What is that? Twenty-five, thirty miles?"

"Twenty," I say. I can see him leaning on the banister, both hands resting on the railing, the life preserver on his left side, the spotlight on his right. "Permission to come aboard."

"Not just yet," he says. There is exactly one Laughing Gull on each of the posts of the landing. "Not just yet."

"I could step over this chain," I say.

"And I could blow your ass back!" he says, and the gulls,

scores of them, laugh hysterically. "I could blow your ass all over this boat!"

"Do you threaten every passenger who walks up?"

"That's just it," he says. "I ain't ever *had* a passenger just *walk up*. You're my first. And look at you! Barefooted! You say you just flew into town—you ain't got no luggage! And what did you do in your britches! Son, we don't have any facilities on board." The gulls erupt in a chorus of guffaws.

"Will you take me across?"

"What time is it?" he says.

"A quarter till six," I say. "Five forty-three."

"Seventeen minutes," he says. "In seventeen minutes," he says. He turns off the spotlight, steps into the wheelhouse, and closes the door.

"What happened?" I say.

"What?" he says. He removes our moorings, and we embark. Each and every last gull takes flight to escort us. They take turns diving into the froth of our wake.

"The battleground!" I say.

"What about it?" he says.

"It's underwater!" I say.

"Sunk," he says. He is a small man, wiry, burned down one side of his body. One half of his face looks like it has melted. His right arm withered. His right eye white.

"It sunk," he says. "This whole part of the country's sunk." He looks at me with his good eye. "Subsidence, they call it. Subsided some ten feet this century. The refineries up the Channel are to blame. They keep pumping out the groundwater. We keep sinking."

He is wearing a captain's cap. "Are you the captain?" I say.

"The pilot?" I look up to the dark windows of the wheelhouse. "I mean, is there someone up there steering this thing?"

"You'll get there," he says. He is smiling. "If I was you, I'd start worrying about what's waiting for me on the other side." He points out into the wake, and I see the dark dorsals in the white froth. Dolphins? Sharks? "I'd put my shoes on," he says, "and I'd tie my laces tight!" He takes off toward the bow, a slight limp in his gait, and I take off after him.

"Why?" I say.

He is standing at the bow, looking out over the water.

"What?"

"I don't think you know where you're going," he says. "I don't think you know what's waiting for you."

It is almost dawn, and I look to the light in the east and see what he sees—not a sunrise, not a sun coming up, but a fire—a big fire burning on the far shore.

"What do you want?" he says.

"To get to the other side," I say.

He laughs. "When the gods want to punish you," he says, "they answer your prayers. Now you understand me. I'm taking you across. I'm taking you to the other side." He takes off his cap and waves it in the air, and the scores of gulls cry. "But me and my gulls," he says, "we ain't waiting. We ain't waiting for you. We're going back. Do you understand?"

"I understand," I say.

"There's nothing out there," he says. "There's no one out there anymore."

"No one?" I say.

"No one in his right mind," he says. *"Degüello,"* he says. "It means revenge, I think. Sweet revenge—something like that—for what the Mexicans did at the Alamo. It used to be a real show-place. The country club section of town. All the oil executives lived out there. Big houses. Big homes."

"I know," I say.

"But not anymore," he says. "Most of those houses are out in the water now. Most of those homes are out in the bay."

"What happened to the people?" I say. "What happened to the families?"

"Most of the old families died off," he says. "Most of them moved away."

"Are they all gone?"

"They ain't *all* gone," he says. "I think there's some hold-outs, but I shit you not, their asses are out in the water! Their asses are out in the bay! They park their cars on the levee road and take boats to their houses!"

"The city's shut the place down," he says, "barricaded the entrances, cut off the utilities, so there might be someone living in those homes, but like I said, no one in his right mind."

It is dawn when the ferry reaches the other side. Each and every last Laughing Gull lands just long enough for us to ease into the landing, for him to lower the chain, for me to step onto the shore before the ferry drifts back into the Channel, and they all take flight again.

"Last chance," he says, the ferry drifting farther. He reaches out with his good arm.

"Thanks for the ride!" I say.

He shakes his head, lifts the chain, and shouts across the water, "You won't like what you find!" He shouts, "Do you know what's waiting for you! Do you know what's over there!"

And I say, not loud enough for him to hear me, I say, "Home."

OLD RIVER

EVERY NIGHT since the storm, a tug pushes a barge loaded with hurricane debris down Old River and into the bay to an island where the trees, limbs, and branches will be burned. Every night, the tug blows its low whistle above the wooden drawbridge, not too far from the bay.

THE MAXWELLS are not home. They are somewhere in Connecticut, visiting their children.

Jessie is in their pool. She hears the tug's whistle. She is bathing. There has been no water for some nine days. She removes her bathing suit. There is no danger of her being seen. There is no electricity.

She brings her own soap, shampoo, a towel. She sits on the steps of the shallow end and rubs a wet bar of soap up her shin. She shaves her legs in the dark.

The deep end is filled with large and small branches. Jessie worries that there are snakes in the bottom of the pool, in the leaves. She wonders if the chlorine will kill them.

The storm blew over Jessie's trees. Her Chinese tallow knocked down a section of the Maxwells' fence. It landed across the diving board, its top branches dipping into the deep end. Her magnolia took down the power lines.

It is warm out. There has been no rain.

The Maxwells do not invite Jessie swimming.

DOWN THE highway, working around the clock, the telephone company is trying to repair the lines. Tornados snapped most of the poles in two. The crosstrees, suspended by the lines, hang off to the side now and swing when there is a breeze. The workmen are transferring the lines from these tops to what is left of the poles.

Every now and then, they touch the right lines together, and all the telephones, up and down the highway, ring.

JESSIE IS washing her hair. There are soapsuds on the surface of the water. She looks up from time to time to make sure no one sneaks up on her.

Somewhere, a telephone is ringing.

She lifts her hair from the water. Is it her phone or the Maxwells'? With both hands, she wipes the soap off her brow. She pushes the lather back and over her head.

The phone rings.

Jessie climbs the steps of the pool. She walks quickly down the tallow. She runs naked across her back yard, reaches through her kitchen window. "Hello?" she says.

There is static on the line. But she can hear voices that sound far away, whispering across the river, from the next county, Louisiana maybe. They are saying things.

She can catch words, phrases sometimes. They are saying, "Please... hope... soon."

MRS. STRAWBRIDGE brings over two margaritas from next door. They are sitting in lawn chairs in Jessie's front yard. The sun has gone down. People from out of town are driving up and down the highway, looking at the hurricane damage.

"I hope they're okay," Mrs. Strawbridge says. "I made them in the dark."

"Thanks," Jessie says. She is wearing one of Travis's khaki hunting shirts. She has folded back the sleeves. "So," she says. She sips her drink and frowns. "When do you expect him?"

Mrs. Strawbridge is wearing an old pink housecoat with a gold sea horse on the pocket. "When he gets here," she says. She is barefooted. "When he drives in that driveway."

All day long, until practically dark, there is the constant whine of chain saws.

Jessie stirs her drink with her forefinger. No ice. She's trying to taste the triple sec, the lime juice. She's trying to taste something in the margarita besides tequila. "Then you don't think he's heard about all this?" she says.

"Oh, he's heard about it, all right," Mrs. Strawbridge says. "But you see, honey, he ain't coming back just because of the storm. I mean, Peck loves me." She laughs. "But he don't love me that much."

Jessie thinks back to when she and Travis went down with them to their house on an island off the coast of Belize. How the dawn came so early. How they fished for tarpon in the mangrove lagoons behind the caye.

Peck is gone about two months out of the year.

A large dog starts barking down by the water. Mrs. Strawbridge looks over her shoulder. "Bear!" she shouts. She takes a deep drink of her margarita. "He's got him a squirrel treed," she says. Both of their yards back up to Old River.

"You haven't seen my little Casper, have you?" Jessie says.

"He's my kitten. My cat. He's a cat now. A small cat. He's white. Travis gave him to me a couple Christmases ago."

"He missing?"

"Since the storm," Jessie says. "You can imagine. He was pretty scared."

"*I* was pretty scared," Mrs. Strawbridge says.

"What with all the noise, the glass breaking. He must have gotten out."

Jessie looks back toward the barking. There are some pecan trees in rows down by the water. Bear is standing up against one of them. Everything else is quiet. The chain saws have stopped.

"Haven't seen him," Mrs. Strawbridge says. "God, I've seen Bear ruin some cats. Pick them up and shake them to pieces. Have you tried the dog pound?"

Jessie sets her drink down on the lawn. She doesn't finish it. She is standing now. "Ma'am?" she says. She is looking into the pecan trees, looking for something white.

"I said, you ought to try the dog pound."

"Sure," Jessie says. "I'll have to drive over and see if they have him." She sticks her hands in her pockets. "I better go on in," she says. "I have a little schoolwork I need to do. Thanks for the drink."

All the windows of the houses are open, some broken. There are leaves stuck to the panes, to the trim of the eaves as if they had been glued there. It's a sticky hot even after dark. There is no breeze.

"My pleasure," Mrs. Strawbridge says.

Jessie's standing at her front door. "If you need anything in the night," she says, "just holler."

There is no one on the highway.

"Oh, honey," Mrs. Strawbridge says, "don't you worry about me." She is saying these things with her back to the houses. "Peck wanted to take old Bear down to the island with him." Jessie is closing her door slowly. "But I told him, I said, 'Hell no, you ain't taking that animal and leaving me here all by my...'"

THE STORM has stalled miles off the coast. It is intensifying in the Gulf. Landfall is expected early in the morning.

Jessie is in her living room, working on a bulletin board for the first day of school. She has moved the furniture to the walls. The coffee table, a couple of chairs. She is on her knees in the middle of the floor.

There is a yellow poster board school bus spread out on the carpet. It is about six feet long. There are animals sitting in the bus, waving out the windows: a rabbit, a raccoon, a little bear, a giraffe. An elephant, wearing a bus driver's cap, sits behind the wheel.

A banner on the side of the bus reads, "Welcome Back."

"Welcome," Jessie says out loud. "Welcome Back. Welcome Back to School."

AT DUSK, the swamps east of Old River are a dark green. The water is the color of coffee, deep enough to pole a bateau through.

Some of the trees in these swamps are dead, bearded with Spanish moss. Some have fallen over, leaving broad-based stumps sticking out of the backwater.

There is little noise until just dark. The whispered flight of a white egret through the cypresses. A far-off pileated drums rotten wood. Crickets. Every now and then, a bass bursts the surface of the water.

The tidal surge from the storm has pushed salt water into

these swamps. The freshwater fish have left. They have gone up Old River for a while, where it is safe. The bream and the sacalait. The gar, the gaspergou.

THE STORM blew one of Jessie's hanging baskets through the picture window in her living room. The bus was blown over, the animals strewn about the room. The rabbit and raccoon are missing.

It is the early afternoon, around one. They have turned the gas back on. She is almost out of water. There is barely an inch left in the bathtub. She makes a small pot of coffee, pours herself a cup.

Jessie stares at the surface of the liquid where the powdered cream spirals slowly counterclockwise. She has seen this pattern before on the weather bulletins. It is an amazing likeness of the time-lapse photographs taken of the hurricane. She watches it. She can see its eye.

Someone knocks on her front door. "Anybody home?" Mrs. Strawbridge.

"Come on in," Jessie says. She walks to the front of her house.

There is a picture of their wedding reception on the top of the television. In it, she is feeding Travis cake. During the storm, the picture was the first thing Jessie went for. She grabbed it and laid it face down so that it wouldn't be blown over and broken.

She picks up the picture and looks into it. Travis is moving his head. His mouth is open. They are both laughing. There is some white icing on his mustache.

"Where are you?"

"Coming," Jessie says. She stands the picture back on the set. Sometimes, she can hear the sound of children on a playground. "Coming," she says.

"There you are," Mrs. Strawbridge says. She is wearing a red nightgown with plastic pearl buttons down the front. Her yard man has come today. There are little pieces of grass on her house shoes.

"You want a shot of coffee?" Jessie says. "I just made a pot."

Mrs. Strawbridge has her hair in curlers. Her eyelids are heavy. "I found your cat," she says.

"Casper?" Jessie says. She walks past Mrs. Strawbridge and into the front yard. "Where is he?"

"The damnedest thing," Mrs. Strawbridge says. "Waking me up every night." She takes Jessie's elbow. "Come on, I'll show you," she says. Jessie can smell the beer on her breath.

They walk across the yard. The lawn chairs are still out from last night. The cicadas, loud in the limbs of the fallen trees, sound electric.

"Do you have him?" Jessie says. She is letting herself be ushered along. The two women have locked elbows.

Mrs. Strawbridge's eyes are almost closed. "Oh, I have him, all right," she says. "In my attic. Been up in my goddamn attic for about a week. Meowing his head off."

"Your attic?" Jessie says. She stops walking.

"Running all over the place like a madman," Mrs. Strawbridge says. She pulls Jessie along walking again.

"You don't think it's a squirrel, do you?" Jessie says. "You know, we've had a squirrel in our..."

"Hell no, it ain't a squirrel," Mrs. Strawbridge says. "I know a goddamn squirrel when I hear one."

THEY ARE standing in the Strawbridge's den. There is a large blue tarpon mounted over the couch, a red fly hooked in its mouth. Three mule deer heads hang in the dining room. White-tail racks line the walls of the den. There is the walnut gun cabinet Travis made for Peck the year before last.

They walk through the den, into the hallway. The door to the attic is a ladder that folds up into the ceiling.

"I just don't see how Casper could have gotten in your attic," Jessie says. "Now, I could see how a..."

They are in the hallway, just outside the master bedroom. Jessie sees the portraits of two young girls above the king-sized bed. Beside these, she sees another portrait, a woman about her age, maybe older. The daughter.

"Come here," Mrs. Strawbridge says. She takes Jessie by the little finger and pulls her into the bedroom so that they will be on the climbing side of the ladder. Then she pulls the cord, opens the attic door. When the ladder is unfolded, it blocks the hallway and cuts them off from the rest of the house.

"He's up here," Mrs. Strawbridge whispers from the top of the ladder.

Jessie peeps her head into the attic. It's hot inside the house with no air conditioning, but in the attic it feels as if there is no air. Mrs. Strawbridge is already bounding off over some other part of the house. She's gonna fall through the ceiling, Jessie is thinking. She's gonna fall right through.

Jessie's eyes adjust to the darkness. Not too far from the attic door, there is a small Christmas tree. Balls, tinsel, a star. Her eyes recognize familiar forms in the dark. Over by the eaves, there is a small girl's bicycle lying on its side. Training wheels.

Mrs. Strawbridge has a glass eye. She and her family were standing on the dock in Texas City. A grain shipment exploded, destroying most of the port. Mrs. Strawbridge lost an eye in the explosion. She lost a daughter, one of the twins.

"Where are you?" Jessie says.

"Over here," Mrs. Strawbridge says, "above the den."

"Give me a second," Jessie says. She starts off in the direction of Mrs. Strawbridge's voice, balancing down the ceiling joists. "This is crazy," she says under her breath. The attic is barely tall enough to stand up in. She's stepping over boxes, holding on to two-by-twelves overhead, straddling air-conditioning ducts.

"Why don't you call him?" Mrs. Strawbridge says.

This is absolutely ridiculous, Jessie's thinking. "Casper?" she almost whispers. "Come here, kitten."

The wind turbines on the roof let in little light. They are turning slowly, making quiet creaking noises.

"Casper!" Mrs. Strawbridge says. "Don't go giving me the silent treatment, now. This is the lady you wake up every night!" She takes off across the attic, crawling over things. "He's usually over here," she says. "Right over my bedroom." She stops beneath a turbine. "Shhh," she says. "Did you hear that?" All that Jessie can see of Mrs. Strawbridge are her curlers, illuminated.

"No," Jessie whispers. She wonders if she can find her way back to the attic door by herself. She's squinting through the darkness into the crevice of the eaves, where she would hide if she were a cat.

"Meow."

Jessie spins around. "Now, I heard that!" she says.

"That was me," Mrs. Strawbridge says. "Meow," she goes.

Jessie's blouse is already completely soaked. She grabs a middle button and fans herself with the shirt, pulling it away from her skin several times quickly. "You don't have any *lights* up here, do you?" she says. "I mean, I couldn't see him if I saw him."

"No," Mrs. Strawbridge says, "but Peck has a humongous flashlight down in his truck." She's over by the door. "I'll run and get it." She's climbing down the ladder. "Be back in a second," she says.

Jessie hears Mrs. Strawbridge fold up the ladder. She hears her close the attic door into the ceiling so that she can pass under it, back into the house. Now it is completely dark.

She hears a boat speeding down Old River. Bear is barking at something down close to the water. Skiers probably. "Shut up!" Mrs. Strawbridge says.

The telephone rings down below.

"Hello," Mrs. Strawbridge says. "Hello? I can barely hear you!"

"Hey!" she says. "Is that you? The lines are bad. I can barely..." Jessie can hear Mrs. Strawbridge shouting these things into the phone.

"We're all safe and sound. High and dry."

Jessie tries to move over to where Mrs. Strawbridge is talking. She hits her head on one of the rafters. "Dammit," she says.

"*I said*, Everything's fine here. It was a big one. Worse than Carla.

"No," Mrs. Strawbridge says. "No, the house is okay. Lots of trees knocked down. The river didn't get up. We still don't have...

"She's all right. She's fine. I was saying, We still don't have any electricity.

"Hello? You there?"

Silence. Jessie wipes the sweat off her face with the wet sleeves of her blouse. She is listening for the back door. She is listening for the door of the garage, the door of the truck.

Jessie hears Mrs. Strawbridge open the front door and then close it. Where is she going?

All is quiet down by the water. The boat has left the river. There is no barking. There is no sound in the house.

What is it that she hears? Is it the cry of a cat? Is it the creaking of the turbines turning slowly in the breeze?

She squints into the darkness. "Casper?" she whispers.

JESSIE SITS and looks across Old River, waiting for the traffic light to change. The wooden drawbridge is only one lane. A farmer is crossing on a tractor. She can see him at the other end of the bridge, some two hundred yards away. He takes his baseball cap off, wipes his brow.

She waits in her orange Volkswagen van. She thinks she can see the bay, the open water. The mouth, not quite a mile away.

There is a bluff on the other side of the river. On the bluff is a white brick building. The animal shelter. The farmer waves to her, the tractor passes, the light turns green.

Jessie loves this bridge. She can smell the creosote on the ties as she crosses it. There are no guardrails. The bridge is not far from the water.

About halfway, there is a small office with stairs down to the river, a boat tied to the stairs. A man in the office operates the drawbridge and the caution arms.

Travis used to take Jessie floundering. They would pull their boat across this bridge.

JESSIE TURNS off the highway, crosses a cattle guard, and pulls into the drive. There are no vehicles parked outside. Part of the aluminum roof has blown off over the bluff. Part is wrapped around a live oak down by the water. She can hear the barking even before she turns off her engine.

She cannot see anyone around. She walks through the front gate. "Anybody here?" she says. On the office door, there is a picture of a puppy. There is a heart drawn above the puppy, a message in the heart. "Take me home with you," it says. She knocks on the office door. She hears a large dog growling.

The shelter is designed like a barn, with a passageway down its middle. Three pens on each side.

Jessie stands in the passageway. "Hello?" she says, and two of the larger dogs start fighting.

She walks quickly over to their pen. A German shepherd and a Doberman. "Hey now!" she says, slapping the gate with her hand. The Doberman has the shepherd by the neck, shaking his head from side to side. They make an eerie sound biting into each other, a growl, a vicious purring. "Stop it!" Jessie says. She kicks the gate hard. She shouts, "Hey!"

The two dogs back away from each other. The shepherd comes to her, its tail wagging, its ear torn. She squats down to look at him. "Now quit that," she says. "Just quit it."

There are two dogs in almost every pen, segregated according to their size. A Chihuahua and a terrier. A basset hound and a dachshund. A small boxer, a beagle. They have all quit barking. The beagle and the terrier are standing with their front paws on the gate, whining. The others are quiet. They are watching her. Don't look in their eyes, Jessie's thinking.

In one pen, a small black puppy lies in the back corner, its head resting on its front paws. Jessie thinks it's a Labrador.

In another pen is a little fyce. He is standing on his hind legs, hopping around in circles. "You're a cutie," Jessie says. She sticks her fingers through the gate so that the fyce can lick them. "Yes sir," she says.

There are clipboards wired to the gates of these pens. On the clipboards are impoundment notices. Under the heading "Animal Impoundment," there are words with boxes beside them:

Given Up Stray Eviction Bite Vicious Live Dead
Under the heading "Disposition of Animal":

Adopted Euthanized Vet Redeemed
A city truck with a cage in the back pulls into the drive. The dog-catcher.

At the bottom of the form, in bold letters,
Animal to be Euthanized:
    ☐ Yes
    ☐ No

"Can I help you?" A young man in his late twenties. Blond, light eyes, tan. He is leading a cocker spaniel on a leash.

"No," Jessie says. "I'm just looking around." She wonders what he's doing working at a place like this. He looks like a lifeguard. "Why don't you separate some of these dogs?" she says.

"Can't," he says. He unlocks the door of the office. "Excuse me a second." He smiles. He has nice teeth. "Don't have any more room," he says from inside. He steps back out, holding a black plastic sack. "Come on," he says to the spaniel. "What with the storm and all," he says. "We're swamped."

He opens the gate of the pen with the Labrador puppy. "Knocking people's fences over." He picks the puppy up by the scruff of the neck and cradles him in his arm. "Jesus," he says, "we're in a no vacancy situation here." He leads the spaniel into the empty pen and closes the gate.

Jessie walks over to pet the puppy. "Hello boy," she says.

"You a teacher?" the young man says.

"Yes," Jessie says. "At Crockett."

"Thought I'd seen you," he says. He shakes the plastic sack open and drops the puppy into it. "I have a sister that goes there. Fourth grade." He sets the sack against the pens.

Jessie frowns down at the sack, then looks into the young man's eyes. He wants to see me react, she's thinking. "How long do you keep these animals?" she says.

"Four days usually," the young man says. "But lately, a couple days. Three days. Then we have to send them down. Depends on how much room we have."

Send them down. "Well, anyway," Jessie says, "I just stopped by to look for a cat. But I don't see any... You don't keep cats, do you?"

"Sure," he says. "They're out back."

They walk down the passageway to the rear of the shelter. Outside, Jessie can see how the river makes a final bend into the bay.

"Here," the young man says. There are three small cages sitting on a long wooden table, up against the back wall. "Holler if you find what you want," he says. "I've got a little work I need to do."

"Thanks," Jessie says. There is no protective roof over the cages, no aluminum patio cover. These cages are on the bay side of the building. Whatever cats were here that night must have caught every bit of the storm.

There are two black kittens with white feet in the first cage. They are not meowing, but crying a constant cry, showing their teeth the way cats do when they are frightened.

She looks to the second cage. "Casper!" she says and opens the cage door. "What are you doing in there?" Casper meows. She reaches in and pulls him out. "Come on," she says. "We're getting you the hell out of here."

The young man walks out of the passageway. "I'm going to the house," he says. "You find one you like?"

"Yes," Jessie says. "Thank you very much." She starts walking for the front gate.

"Now, hold on, school teacher," he says. He is standing so that she cannot get by him. "You can't just walk in here, grab a animal, and run."

"I'm sorry," Jessie says. "I didn't know. What do I need to do?"

The young man smiles at her. It's a mean smile. "It *is* past my closing time," he says.

Jessie doesn't say anything. She's rubbing Casper behind the ears.

"But what the hell," he says. "You know, I've always *admired* school teachers." He laughs. "Really!" he says. "Now, for starters, let me have this little fellow." He reaches over and takes Casper. He walks to the empty cage. "I just need some of this information."

"I'm sorry to keep you," Jessie says.

"There's a Miss Bingham," he says. He's looking at Jessie as he's taking the impoundment notice off the clipboard. "A fourth grade teacher," he says. "My sister's name's Bonnie."

"Bonnie," Jessie says.

"That's right," he says. "She's a smart girl." He looks at the form. "Whoa!" he says. "You can't take this cat."

"Why not?"

"He's done been adopted," the young man says. "Look." He hands her the impoundment notice.

Across the top of it is written, "Hold until Monday. For C. Fisher."

"You can have any of these other ones," he says. In the third cage, a calico.

"I don't *want* any of the other ones," Jessie says. "That's my cat. He was given to me as a present."

"Well, I tell you what you do," he says. "You come back here Monday morning and talk to a Mr. Burdett. You bring your proof of ownership..."

"What proof of ownership?" Jessie says. "He's *mine!* He's *my* cat!" She points to a line on the form. "You see that?" she says. "Location of pickup: Old River Road. That's me. That's where I live!"

"He's not your cat no more," the young man says. He isn't

smiling now. "As of Monday, he belongs to this Mr. Fisher. And don't go raising your voice to me, school teacher! We ain't in your classroom." He takes the form from her.

"Besides," he says, "look at the date here. We picked this cat up August 18! Now, that's more than a week ago. And I've already told you we don't keep *no* animal for more than four days." He sticks Casper back in the cage and slams the door so hard it frightens the black kittens.

"Let me tell you how it is," the young man says, sitting back on the long wooden table, his arms crossed in front of him. "Mr. C. Fisher is the brother-in-law of Mr. Burdett. Mr. C. Fisher tells Mr. Burdett to keep an eye out for a kitten for his daughter. Daughter's birthday's Monday. Mr. Burdett puts a hold on this cat for some... nine days now."

He places his hands on the table on both sides of him. "It's this simple," he says. "*That* is a dead cat. It should be a dead cat. You're damn lucky it ain't out there somewhere underneath the bay with all its buddies."

Jessie looks past him to Casper in the cage. She looks into the young man's blue eyes. "Mr. Burdett," she says.

"That's right," he says.

She turns and walks down the passageway, through the shelter. The fyce stands on his hind legs and yelps. She hears the young man walking close behind her.

When she gets to the front gate, she looks back. The young man is standing in the front yard of the shelter. He is swinging the black plastic sack back and forth at his side. He says, "You come on back here Monday, you hear?"

Jessie looks at the sack. She smiles. "Oh, I'll come back, all right," she says.

DURING THE storm, Jessie stood at her back door and watched
the wind push waves into her yard. She watched the whitecaps,
the treetops whipping.

She held Travis's hunting flashlight, and every now and then,
she turned it on and searched her back yard for the river to see
if it was rising.

The storm brought a type of lightning Jessie had never seen
before, a lightning without streaks that lit up the sky for seconds
at a time, so that she could see the river, and the swaying trees
across the river, and the tractor parked beneath the trees.

IT IS dark now. The light is green. Jessie crosses the bridge slowly.
A light is on in the small office, but she cannot see anyone in there
as she passes. Jessie speeds up on the back side of the bridge.
She turns her lights off, coasts up the highway, across the cattle
guard, and into the drive.

The animal shelter does not have any outside lighting. There
is only a long fluorescent bulb running down the length of the
passageway.

Jessie gets out of her Volkswagen. She has brought a pair of
Travis's wire cutters just in case. But there is no chain. There is
no lock on the gate. Who would break into a dog pound?

"Get in," Jessie says in a whisper, "and get the hell out of
there." Everything is quiet. She cannot hear the river. There are
no cars on the highway.

She walks quickly through the shelter, out back to where the
cages are. She opens the second one down. "Let's go," she says
to Casper.

She heads for the van. All the dogs are awake. They are watching her. Don't look at them. In the far pen, one of the dogs is

jumping up and down. The little fyce. He is dancing for her. There is a circle drawn in magic marker on the impoundment notice:

Animal to be Euthanized:

☑Yes

☐ No

Jessie opens the gate of the pen. "You're coming with me," she says. The fyce runs to her and jumps into the air. She catches him at her hip.

She is holding Casper under her left arm, the fyce under her right. She turns to look down the passageway one last time. She sees all those eyes.

"Oh Jesus," she says.

JESSIE STARTS the van. She looks up the highway. No one. "Good," she says and takes off down the drive. So far, so good.

There is no one on the bridge. Jessie's hoping to just sneak across it quietly, not wake the man in the office. It's late. Lightning bugs drift over Old River. A cool breeze comes in from the bay.

The beagle jumps up in the passenger seat and thrusts his head out the window. His mouth open, his tongue dangling.

They are on the bridge. Jessie's holding Casper in her lap. Someone starts growling behind her. She turns around. "Shhh," she says. "Hush that up." The entire back of the van is filled with wagging tails. "Jesus Christ," Jessie says.

It is the shepherd growling. He is looking out the side window. He sees something in the darkness. It's the bridge, Jessie's thinking. It's making him nervous. And then she sees it, something big and dark coming down the river. "Oh shit," she says and stomps the gas pedal. The tug blows its whistle.

The caution arms lower. The basset hound, sitting on the floorboard beside her, begins to howl to the tug. The drawbridge opens.

Jessie stops behind the caution arm. She covers her face with both hands. "No," she says. She opens her fingers and looks through them at herself in the rearview mirror. "No, no, no."

The office is on the other side of the opening. The barge passes through slowly. Jessie sticks her thumbs in her ears at the next blast. Casper jumps out the window and takes off down the bridge.

"Casper," she says, opens the door and starts running after him. He is heading for the highway. "Casper!" she shouts. She is halfway to the shore.

Jessie hears a horn honking, a constant horn. She stops, turns around, and there is a trail of dogs behind her. First, there is the shepherd, then the beagle, the basset. Behind them, the dachshund and the terrier. The Chihuahua is looking over the side of the bridge at the water.

The horn is coming from her van. It is the fyce. He's standing in the driver's seat, his front paws on the steering wheel, on the horn. He's barking through the windshield at the tug as it clears the drawbridge.

Jessie looks down the bridge to the highway. Casper is a small white dot disappearing into the darkness. Soon, the man will close the drawbridge. Soon, he will raise the caution arms. Maybe a car is waiting on the other side of the river.

Should she start running? Should she start running for Casper before he completely disappears? Should she turn and grab what dogs she can and head for the van?

She is just standing there in a circle of dogs. They are all looking at her. The bridge is closing. The horn has stopped. The fyce is now outside the van, barking at the tug as it vanishes into the black of the river.

Jessie looks up the bridge, down the highway. Should she?

SHE HAS been thinking of him this evening. She has been thinking of how they talked of saving up and buying the land across Old River so that they could wake up in the mornings and look out at their yard sloping down to the water, and across the river would be theirs, too. They could just wake up and sit down at the breakfast table, look out as far as they could see, and it would be theirs. They had talked of how, on his days off, he could clear it of brush, thin some of the trees.

She is thinking of the day she came home from visiting her mother in Waco. She carried her suitcase around into the back yard, and there he was, across Old River, on his father's tractor, mowing. And when she walked down their yard to the water, he waved at her.

He rented a brush hog and cleared the brush. He thinned out some of the trees, cutting down the mimosa and sweet gum, leaving the large live oak. He used a chain saw and cut the trees off about three feet from the ground. He cut the trees, made a pile, made a big bonfire. And on that evening, after dinner, they sat at the table with all the lights in the house off, and had a beer, and watched the fire glow late into the night.

He used a tractor, wrapped a towing chain around the tree stumps, and pulled them from the ground. He had been working on the stump of the big magnolia which had been killed by lightning.

She is thinking of the day she came home from school, and his truck was in the driveway. She put her books, her purse, on the drainboard and looked out the kitchen window, and there was the dead magnolia stump, and there was the tractor, lying on its side.

MRS. STRAWBRIDGE has gone to bed. Peck's kerosene lantern is not in the kitchen window. Only the fog man is on the highway, the man who sprays for mosquitos. As he passes, his spray climbs Jessie's lawn and obscures things.

Jessie is sitting in her van, in her driveway. She has been sitting here for some time, listening to the slowing tick of the engine cooling. She is not crying now. School will start the day after tomorrow.

She watches the mist of the fog man. She cannot see her lawn chairs, her mailbox by the highway. She takes a deep breath, pulls the key from the ignition, and gets out of the van. She wants to walk out into the mist, slowly, but it is already thinning.

Jessie takes a flashlight whenever she goes out after dark. She shines it on her house. Her front door is open. But didn't she close it before she left? Didn't she lock it?

She shines the flashlight down the long hall. There are no closets opened, no drawers dumped on the floor. She should not walk into a dark, open house.

It just doesn't matter, Jessie's thinking. They can have everything. She walks quickly into the house to the television set, grabs the picture frame, and shines the flashlight on the two of them. She holds the picture to her stomach and scans the den with her light. The back door is open. She should get out of this house.

She looks out the back door, down her dark yard to the water. There is something across the river. She turns her flashlight off, jumps when the telephone rings. There is something in the trees, down close to the ground. The phone rings. She walks over, feels for it in the dark, "Hello."

There is no answer. There is only the sound of a quiet storm of static.

Jessie walks over, with the receiver, to the back door and looks across Old River. It is the moon, a late moon rising, large at the horizon, shining through the trunks like a fire in the trees.

"Hello?" she says. There is a quiet sound blowing through the lines, like a message carried by the wind from far away, as if someone's whispering to her, saying her name.

Jessie's listening, straining into the receiver. "Travis," she whispers. "Travis?" she says.

♦♦♦♦♦♦♦♦♦♦♦♦♦♦♦♦♦♦♦♦♦♦♦♦♦♦♦

THE BOTTOM

═══════════════════════════════

OLD RIVER BOY ESCAPES DEATH

NOTHING IS happening, no traffic, so Seth is in the men's room, sitting on the commode, digging a hole in the wall with a Phillips head screwdriver. He's already started on two other holes, but after running back and forth to the ladies' room, he's decided that the holes won't come out at the right spot so he's started on this one.

There is a young woman in the ladies' room. She has dark hair, almost black, past her shoulders. She has a dark tan. She is wearing a white sleeveless cotton dress.

Seth watches the young woman remove the white dress. He watches her pull it up and over her head. She is standing there before him, naked. She is turning slowly so that he can see where her tan stops and then starts. Seth is looking at her abdomen where a faint line of hair grows up toward her navel.

He digs for a while until the hole gets deeper than his screwdriver is long, and he has to stop.

Out on the highway, everything is quiet. Just about everyone has driven over to Hog Island. Traffic will pick up again when the sun starts going down.

Seth walks around front to the station office to get a longer screwdriver. Everything is just about this dead every day at this time. The sun is working its way back behind the station. Seth gets the key out of the cash drawer and unlocks the candy machine and examines all the candies and eats the ones that are pretty close to stale.

He has a big nut bar stuck in his mouth, and he's sucking on it, tearing through the tool drawers, when he runs across a brand-new piece of yellow chalk still in its wrapper. This is the chalk Mr. Moss uses to draw circles around leaks in inner tubes. Seth takes it outside and tears the wrapper off and starts looking for something to draw on. He looks up and down the highway, and there isn't anybody coming, so he decides to trace the shadow the horse makes on the cement pavement in front of the station.

There is a horse on the roof of the station. It isn't a real horse. It's a sign, a red horse with wings with a thin red neon bulb around its edges to light it up at night. Anybody driving by on the highway can see it. As a matter of fact, it was the first thing Seth saw when he and his dad pulled into the Bottom and turned off the highway, down the road that runs beside the station.

Mr. Moss owns the trailer park down that road where they are living. Seth's dad does maintenance work around the park in the afternoons for extra pay. He also talked Mr. Moss into letting Seth work at the station on the weekends.

And on the afternoon that Seth learned he had the job, he got his bicycle out after supper and rode it down to the station and stopped right under the canopy next to the island with the gas pumps and the air hose. He watched the cars all headed north away from the bay.

This is a pretty dingy-looking station, Seth was thinking. It smelled like old rubber tires. The glass on one of the pumps had been broken so that he could reach in with his thumb and turn the dollar dials. $99.00 worth of regular. And every time a car passed on the highway, Seth stomped the hose with his heel, and a bell in the grease rack went *dink*.

Pyramids of motor oil cans lined the large front windows of the filling station office. The windows were so dirty that Seth had to clean a place to look through. He could see a candy machine, a cash register, an ashtray overflowing with cigarette butts.

There was a calendar for the year before last hanging on the door to the grease rack. On the calendar was a picture of a barefoot blonde with pigtails sitting on a white wooden fence. The woman was holding an oil filter. She was wearing an unbuttoned red and white checkered cowboy shirt. "Shithouse mouse!" Seth said. He was pressing his nose against the window. The woman was smiling at him. He *had* to work at this station. "How much do goddamn oil filters cost, anyway?" he said.

OLD RIVER BOY WINS SERVICE AWARD
AT AREA FILLING STATION

I CAN wash the windows, empty the ashtrays, sweep out the office, Seth was thinking. I can have this place cleaned up in a week.

Everything was pretty dingy-looking except for maybe the horse on the roof with the thin red neon bulb. It looked cleaner than everything else, Seth thought. Newer. And even as he was watching it, the horse turned itself on.

Seth rode his bike back behind the station and put his kickstand down and climbed up on the big tank that had KEROSENE written on it and jumped up on the roof. He nosed all over the place up there, saving the horse for last, and found a bunch of bottle caps, a couple of beer bottles, an old rotten radiator hose, and a plastic doll without a head, without any clothes.

The horse was about as tall as one of the small Shetland ponies he had ridden once when the circus came to town back when they were living in Orange. Seth flung his leg over it and sat on it, back behind the wings.

The sun had just about gone down, and all that was left was shining on the other old station across the highway and the golden field beside it. Every now and then, a breeze would come in from the bay, and it would look like the whole field was moving. Seth was just sitting there watching the field move, the whole river bottom move, and when anybody driving by on the highway looked up at him, he'd just wave at them.

THERE IS a phone booth on the corner. Seth has watched it and watched the people talking on it. One day, he ran out and got the number off the phone and carried it back inside in his head and wrote it on the wall just above where the station phone hung.

From time to time, someone would pull into the station to use the phone and park over by the rest rooms. And Seth, if he wasn't fixing a flat or changing somebody's oil, would hurry and dial the number and let it ring just before the person's hand touched the receiver and watch them jump. Seth would watch them watching the phone, watch them reach for the receiver and finally answer it, "Hello?"

And he'd say, "What do you want?"

And the person would say something like, "Pardon me?"

And he'd say, "Don't give me that 'Pardon me' crap! This is the third time today you've called and woke me up, and I want it to stop!"

Most of the time, the people would hang up and run back to their car and not even use the phone and drive off.

SETH LOVED to call people on the phone. He loved to call the Chicken Shack in town on Commerce and Main and ask the old woman who worked there, who drooled, he'd ask her, "Do you have chicken legs?"

And she'd say, "Yes." "Yes," she'd say.

And he'd say, "I bet you walk funny."

Or call the market and ask old man Hasty about pig's feet.

Or call the old folks' home, and when the receptionist answered the phone, he'd play like he couldn't hear her, and he'd say, "Hello?"

And she'd say, "Hello?"

And he'd say, "Hellooo! I can't hear you! Hello?"

And she'd say, "Hello, hello?"

The thing was to see how many hellos he could milk out of her before she hung up. The record was twelve.

OLD RIVER YOUTH ESCAPES KILLER

SETH IS sitting up on the roof, looking at the abandoned filling station across the highway. Most of the windows have been boarded up. The pumps disconnected. These two stations are the only buildings the two miles south of town on the highway through the Bottom to the bay. Seth is sitting up on the horse waiting for it to move, waiting for its shadow to move so that he can run down and finish his tracing of it.

Yesterday afternoon, there had been too many cars coming in all at once for him to finish it. He had completed the body and the wings and was just about to begin on the head when the traffic started coming in.

Seth is waiting for the precise moment when the shadow fits perfectly into the picture he has already drawn. He is just sitting there, watching Wilson's station, thinking,

OUTSMARTS KIDNAPPER

OUT IN front of the station, hovering over the Bottom, there are thousands of dragonflies. The air is thick with them. They are watching Seth from across the way.

Seth is thinking, There are too many of them. Soon, they will spill across the highway. Soon, he will have trouble breathing.

He grabs the reins and flies the horse into them. He watches it gnash them like they gnash mosquitos.

OLD RIVER—Sunday afternoon, on that lonely strip of highway south of town, there was an example of extreme...

A CAR pulls into the station and parks over by the rest rooms. Seth jumps off the horse, hurries off the roof, and runs around the other side of the station into the office. The car has orange out-of-state plates.

Seth kneels down behind the cash register and watches a man get out of the car, go through his pockets for some change, and start walking for the phone booth.

The man is wearing shorts! Not only that, the shorts have goofy-looking flowers all over them.

Seth has never seen a grown man wearing shorts before. He crawls over to the wall and dials the number of the phone in the booth. He can peek in between the cash register and the candy machine and see the booth from where he's kneeling. He hears the phone start ringing. He sees the man stop in his tracks and look all around and then finally step into the booth.

The phone rings.

"Hello?" the man says.

"Listen very close," Seth whispers. "This is a emergency."

"What?" the man says.

"Help me," Seth whispers.

"Who is this?" the man says.

"Please!"

"O.K." the man says. "O.K."

"Do you see that station?" Seth says. He's trying to sound like he's crying. He sees the man look in his direction, and he ducks down behind the cash register. "No," he says. "Not that one! The one across the highway."

"Sure," the man says. "I see it."

"You just gotta help me!" Seth says. There is an old empty mousetrap underneath the table.

"Is this a gag?" the man says.

"No, this ain't no gag!" Seth says. "I'm being held prisoner over here by a crazy old man. And he's been beating me up. You still there?"

"I'm still here," the man says. "I'm going to help you. Don't you worry. But where's this guy now? This man?"

"He's ... got me locked up in this back room. I guess he went outside for a minute. You can't see him anywhere, can you?"

Seth sees the man step outside the booth and look at Wilson's station. "No," the man says. "I can't see him anywhere."

"Good," Seth says. "Then maybe he's gone for a while."

"What can I do?" the man says.

"I wish you could come over here and kick these doors in. I'm tied up with these ropes, you see. But this old man's got a gun, and if he comes back and finds you here, he's liable to shoot you."

"Do you want me to call someone?"

"Yeah," Seth tells him. "Why don't you call the police. This man's been hitting me," Seth's pretending he's crying. "And he's been ... What's that?"

"What!" the man says.

"That's him! He's coming back in. Hurry, call the police!" Seth holds the receiver out at the end of his arm. "No, sir!" he says. "I ain't been calling nobody. I . . ." He drops the receiver and kicks the trash can around. He screams. And then he hangs up.

Seth sees the man fly out of the booth and stare at Wilson's station, wiping his hands on his shorts. He sees the man start digging in his pockets and run back into the booth.

Seth walks over and sits in the chair beside the candy machine and starts chuckling. Pretty soon, the police car will get here, and the man in the goofy shorts will walk across the highway like a hero. Seth tells himself that he'll save all his serious laughing for then, if they come, if that's who the man is calling.

And sure enough, within five minutes, here come not one police car, but two, tearing up the highway, skidding into Wilson's driveway with their lights flashing.

Of course, Seth knows, and he knows the policemen know that old man Wilson has been dead for a long time and that nobody is ever in that old station except hobos or winos who crawl in a back window to stay warm or dry on some nights. Of course, the flowerdy shorts man doesn't know this, and that makes it even funnier.

There are three of them: two in one car and one in the other. Seth watches them jump out of their cars and bunch together and start checking the bullets in their guns. The man by the booth waves and shouts across the highway, "I'm the one who called! That's the place, all right! He's in there!"

Two of the policemen flatten themselves up against the wall on both sides of the front door, and the third one, the tallest one, kicks on the door five or six times until it finally opens, and he runs in, limping.

This is all Seth can take. He starts laughing and clapping his hands. He'd made it all up! He'd made it up and now they were acting it out right there in front of him. Now he knows what it means when somebody says that they're laughing until they're crying. Seth's crying, but he's laughing.

He's laughing right up until he hears the screaming and the glass breaking across the way, when he sees a man, an oldish man, get to his feet and start running off across the Bottom, when two of the policemen run around the corner and shout at the man to stop with their pistols lowered.

Seth only wants to see the man, watch the man escape, but when he hears the shots, all he can see are the pistols jumping, barking at something trying to get away.

Everything is quiet again. The policemen, standing over something in the field. The man in the flowerdy shorts, walking slowly across the highway.

Seth's still wiping at his eyes, but the tears keep coming. He even tries blinking hard to make everything clear again.

He looks at the station clock. It's a little before seven on a Sunday. He wonders if it'll be all right to close the station a little early. It doesn't matter, he's thinking. Mr. Moss will fire him for this anyway. He wonders if he'll probably get arrested for playing on the phone.

Seth takes the bills out of the cash register and sticks them in the Bible underneath Mr. Moss's coffee cup. He pulls the door down to the grease rack and locks it and locks the front door. Everything is so blurry he has trouble seeing the holes to put the keys in.

He doesn't take the readings off the meters on the pumps. He doesn't lock the pumps. He doesn't even wash down the pavement like he's supposed to every day before he leaves.

There is the shadow on the pavement, and there is the picture he traced yesterday, the body and the wings. The sun has gone down some since he was up on the roof. The shadow has moved some three feet so that the head is much too high for the body he has drawn. If he finished it now, it would look more like a dragon than a pretty red horse with wings.

The policemen are back inside Wilson's station, looking for something.

Seth starts walking across the highway. As he's walking, he's thinking, about what has happened, other stories he can tell the policemen.

Maybe he won't tell them. Maybe he'll just walk on past Wilson's on the highway and just keep on going.

He walks over between the two police cars, the lights still flashing on top. He's really crying now.

Seth just doesn't want to think about it. He just doesn't want to think about if it's his fault that the man got killed. He closes his eyes to it and sticks it underneath some things in his mind and keeps it hid.

The tallest policeman walks out Wilson's front door and looks across the highway. He's holding an old telephone, its disconnected cord dragging the pavement. He's about to turn and walk back inside when he sees Seth standing beside one of Wilson's old gas pumps.

"Here he is!" he shouts and drops the phone and runs over to Seth and grabs him by both shoulders and shakes him. "Where in the hell you been, boy!" he says. "You had us worried."

The other policemen come running out the front door with the flowerdy man.

Seth's trying to sniffle up all his sniffles so that he can answer him, but he can't even swallow. He hears the flowerdy shorts man say, "That's him!" just like he knows the story.

"Are you O.K.?" the tallest policeman says. The other policemen kneel beside him. "Are you?"

Seth's mind is working. There's a frown on his face like he's concentrating on something, like he's trying to focus on it.

"Don't you worry about a thing," the tallest policeman says. "We got that old bastard out back. He was trying to get away." Across the highway, in the booth, the telephone starts ringing. "Settle down now. Everything's gonna be all right."

One of the other policemen asks him, "Now, why don't you tell us what happened?"

Seth can hear a siren screaming throughout the Bottom. He is looking past the policemen, across the highway. Under the canopy, the red horse is pawing at the pavement. Its head nodding, its wings nervous. Seth opens his mouth, and nothing comes out.

◆ ◆

HAZARD

WE WERE playing the Chambers course, the seventh
hole, a five par. We had started early that morn-
ing, and there was still dew on the greens so that it was hard to
putt.

I was up. I teed up my shot, took three practice swings, and
then hit it about a hundred yards. All my drives are pretty shitty
like that. They don't go very far, and they don't get very high, but
they usually always stay in the fairway.

It was Stu's shot. He stuck his tee in the ground and gave me
a mini-lecture on what I was doing wrong: not teeing my ball up
high enough. He took a practice swing and then sliced it about a
hundred yards into the woods.

I didn't say a word. I was standing there watching him, pinch-
ing my side just above the belt to keep from smiling.

Stu was looking at almost the exact spot where the ball entered
the woods, looking forlorn as if something had just eaten one of
his pets. He reached into his pocket and pulled out another ball
and took an illegal Mulligan.

"Sure," I said. "Go ahead."

He carefully placed his ball on the tee, slowly addressed the
ball, took a practice swing, and then hit it like a center fielder. The
ball hit a pine tree about fifty feet out to the right. It rolled back
in our direction, back on the tee box, pretty close to where his

tee was. Stu reached down and picked up the ball and inspected it like maybe it was defective.

I was standing there biting an inch out of the inside of my cheek. I was trying to concentrate on the trees at the far end of the fairway, trying to act as if I hadn't seen him muff it. I could barely see the pin, the red flag hanging straight down. There wasn't a breeze. I could remember playing in the woods not too far from there, before we moved to the city, playing Houdini, the magician.

I was always Houdini. Stu said it was a big honor. Some days, Mama would drive into Beaumont, shopping with Mrs. Fisher, and Stu would have to babysit me. We would wake up real early on those mornings, and Stu and Bubba Nelson would take me way out in the woods to their clubhouse and tie me to this chair. Then they'd tell me that I was Harry Houdini, the greatest magician that ever lived, and that if I concentrated real hard, I could untie myself and escape. They usually came back for me in the afternoon, about the time Mama would be getting home, arguing between them who was going to be Houdini next.

What they didn't know was that after the first couple years, I learned how to untie myself and followed them all over the neighborhood and spied on them, found all their secret hideouts. Then I'd run back when they'd start coming for me and tie myself up again.

STU WAS finally ready. He very carefully placed the ball on the tee, assumed the proper stance (without his club), shouted "Fore," swooped down with his right hand and grabbed the ball like a third baseman barehanding a grounder, and threw it about as far as my drive.

I didn't say anything. Stu's my older brother. Sometimes, he gets pretty pissed.

HE WAS usually a good golfer, but that day he got hexed early. When you're as good at golf as we are, you don't want to start off the first couple holes playing too well because we've decided that God gets pissed at you and starts screwing you up, puts a hex on you. Any golfer will tell you. You start playing great on the first two or three holes, and then you start trying to concentrate on what you're doing right, and then it gets to the point that you can't even *hit* the ball.

The first hole was a four par. Stu parred it. The second hole was a difficult four par with a hard dogleg right. He had a great drive and an amazing approach shot that landed about fifteen feet from the hole. He could two-putt, and he'd have another par. He one-putted. He got a birdie. When he pulled his ball out of the hole, he looked at me kind of sorry that he'd made such a good putt, shook his head and said, "I'm fucked now."

Stu was in a good mood. He was always in a good mood as long as he was winning.

"Yeah," I said, "you'd better just go back over and sit in the car for the rest of the day. God's not even gonna let you hit another ball in the fairway."

The third hole was a five par. He got a twelve. On the next hole, he had to take a penalty stroke for hitting his ball out of bounds. It was a four par, and he got an eight.

It was the fifth hole, and he was already saying things like, "This is a wasted goddamn day" and "Next time, don't call me. I don't care anything about playing this game again. Don't call me! You hear?"

Stu usually said all that kind of stuff to hurt my feelings or to make me start screwing up too. Sometimes, he could get pretty nasty.

"It's the clubs," I told him. There was a lot on his mind. It was his birthday. He had just turned thirty, and that was bugging him. But I knew there was something else.

For his birthday, Beck gave him a new set of clubs. I gave him two boxes of balls. When I came over that morning, he gave me his old set.

"It's the clubs," I said. We were walking with pull carts. It was already hot as a son of a bitch and quiet. All you could hear were the cicadas and an occasional golf ball bouncing off a tree.

"Here," I said. "You want to use your old clubs?"

"No," he said.

"Come on, you can use them if you want."

"What?" he said. His mind was far off on something else. Something was eating on him. I could tell, and I was pretty sure I knew what it was.

"Sure you don't want to? Use your old clubs? Sure?"

He stopped walking. He turned around and looked me in the eye and said, "No. Now would you just shut up! Just shut the fuck up, and I might be able to play!" He started walking again for the fifth tee. He had a pretty blue and silver golf bag that the old man had given him. I had his old reject.

"Jesus," I said. "I'm sorry. I just thought you might have better *luck* playing with your old clubs."

I had never beaten him at golf. Come to think of it, I had never beaten him at any game that meant a lot to him. Except chess.

He taught me how to play when I was in kindergarten (anyway, that's what Mama tells everyone). I only remember that I was real young and that he would fool's mate me about every game.

I can still see him sliding his queen slowly across the board and knocking my king from the table. He'd grin and say, "Checkmate, Scrote! What you need is a *lot* of practice." He'd laugh, get up from the table, kick the screen door open, and go outside.

One Christmas, some thirteen years later, after a lot of practice, I came home from college, and we played a game that lasted over two hours, and I beat him. I didn't jump up and down on the table, and I didn't knock his king from the board. I just sat there and looked him in the eye and said, "You lose." We never played chess again.

THE FIFTH hole was the kind of hole that golfers have nightmares about. It was a three par with a water hazard in front that formed a horseshoe around the green. There was no doubt in my mind that of all the holes of the Chambers course, the fifth was God's favorite. I had never seen a human clear that water.

Stu and I had a standing bet on which of us could get closer to the green with our first shot. Both of us brought a ten dollar bill and a special ball, an old gnarled one, one we didn't mind losing. The best strategy that I had ever seen used on that hole was teeing the ball close to the ground, closing your eyes, and swinging.

Stu usually won the bet. He usually landed closer to the green in the water than I did. That day, considering the way he was playing, I knew I could get closer. And I knew that he knew it. It would be interesting to see if he would bring up the bet.

"O.K., Scrote," he said. (That was my nickname. That was short for "Scrotum." That was Stu's favorite. His old school friends used to call me that when I was little. My real name is Richard so when I was in public, it was a more formal, "Hey Dick! How's it hanging?" A lot of thought always went into the creation of those names. Back then, I had a few for him too that I'd use when I wanted to get the dog shit beat out of me. Big brothers are wonderful. Everyone should have about a hundred of them.)

"O.K., Scrote," he said. "What's the bet? Ten big ones? You're up." I pulled a seven iron out of my bag. "All right," I said. "This is your idea, now. If you lose, don't go screaming at me all afternoon."

"Come on, little brother," he said, "which of us is *the loser?*"

"Fuck you," I said.

"Don't nut up, now. Don't hit it in the water."

I was concentrating on the green. No, I was concentrating about fifty or a hundred yards past the green. There were some ducks in the hazard. They were swimming around, quacking.

Stu said, "Hey, Scrote! You want me to go get those ducks out of the water? I'd hate for you to kill one of them."

I was concentrating on the cliffs of Dover. I was standing on the shore at Dunkirk. It was just a nice, simple seven iron over the Channel. I took a practice swing.

Stu said, "Hey Scrotum! I just saw an SPCA van pull up. The driver's got some binos on you. He said he's gonna sue your asshole if you get anywhere near one of those baby duckies."

I was listening to every single quack of the ducks. I was hoping the mother would somehow raise one of her wings and say, "Shhh, babies! That man over there is about to hit. Let's be real quiet!"

Stu was leaning up against a magnolia tree going, "Quack, quack-quack."

I had a great idea. I pretended that Stu was real little, that he was buried up to his neck, and that the ball was his little head saying, "Quack-quack, quack-quack." I swung as hard as I could. The ball headed right for the water like a line drive, but when it got there, it skipped twice on the surface and landed on the fringe of the green.

Stu was just looking at me and shaking his head. "You lucky little bastard," he said. He pulled a club out of his bag. "By the way," he said, "you are coming tonight, aren't you?"

"Sure," I said. "I thought I might bring a date if that's all right with you."

"A date!" he said. "That's fine with me, little brother, *if* you think you can handle her. But I don't want you getting a hard-on right in the middle of my birthday party." He laughed.

"You want to double that bet?" I said.

He stopped laughing. "You got it," he said.

The ducks were going wild. They were really quacking it up, trying to get out of the water. They had realized that they were in the line of fire.

Stu drew back and hit a beautiful shot that landed almost exactly in the center of the water hazard.

I was about to let out a good laugh that we could both share when he kicked a large divot out of the ground and shouted, "Son of a bitch!"

Then I said something I didn't think before saying, but I said to make him feel better, which it didn't. I said, "Come on, Stu. It's just a game."

"No!" he said. He spun around and pointed his finger at me. "No, it's not just a goddamn game! And the sooner you realize that, the better off you'll be."

"I just don't see you letting it ruin your day."

And he said, "You don't see it because you don't understand. You never have had and never will have what it takes to win."

"Let's just get nasty," I told him.

"That's what it takes sometimes," he said. "It takes getting nasty. And if I don't teach you anything else, I want you to learn how important it is to come out on top."

FOR STU, it had always been too important. He used to love to play tennis with some of his high school friends and stomp the shit out of them. He got off to that. Of course, nobody played with him more than once, and finally, one by one, his friends left him.

Stu never bragged. I'm not saying that. But he could play you, and he could look you in the eye and still stomp you at damn near any sport you could name.

It was totally because of this that I loved to beat him. Sure, there were times when I was younger when I'd run to Mama after he'd beaten me, but those times passed, and I decided no matter how long it took me, no matter how much I had to suffer, that of the two of us, one day, he would have to admit to himself that I was the winner.

ONE DAY we were jousting, and he split my head open. We were playing knights of the Round Table. He was Arthur (he was always Arthur), and I was Lancelot. Of course, whoever got dibs on being Arthur was guaranteed victory. Arthur always won. He had Excalibur. *Almost* always.

We didn't have steeds or armor so we used bicycles. Bicycles were the steeds, and because you couldn't hold both lance and shield and steer your steed, you needed a squire, a steed steerer. The squire steered and ducked his head to keep clear of the action and pedaled like a bastard. Both of you sat on the banana seat. The squire sat in front. For shields, we used garbage can lids. For lances, commode plungers.

We followed normal jousting rules. Both squires took the

steeds to the opposite ends of the street. Then each knight raised his lance high in the air and screamed. The squires started pedaling, building up speed, and the knights lowered their lances, preparing for the attack.

As in regulation jousting, you tried to stick your lance to your opponent's shield and then pull it away from him. Then on the next pass, you could poke him or his squire in the head with your lance and knock them off their steed.

On that particular pass, Stu stuck his lance to my shield, but as it happened, I pulled it free from his grip. The squires turned for another pass, and Stuart had only a shield. I told my squire I wanted a fast pass. I threw down my shield, grabbed the squire around the neck with my free arm, and shouted, "Let's go!" I got my lance ready. (That was another good thing about those plungers. You could swing them like a battle ax if you wanted. That was in the rules.) I was going to behead Stu or his squire. When we met, I was preparing to hit his squire in the throat when Stu crashed his shield into the side of my head.

I spent something like a week in the hospital.

STU WAS quiet for the rest of the nine. I didn't want him quiet. When he got quiet, he quit trying.

As we walked to the sixth hole, the ducks were regrouping, recuperating from the shelling.

I told him the story about the judge and the geese. There was this judge from Georgia or Virginia or somewhere who was playing a game with his doctor friend. They were betting something like a hundred dollars a hole, and it all came down to the eighteenth. They were even. That hole had a water hazard with a lot of geese in it. Anyway, the judge was putting, and one of the geese slipped up and pecked him on the ass. I think he screwed up his putt pretty bad, knocked it off the green and into the water. Then he said they all started laughing at him, the geese I mean, kind of honking, so he hauled off with his putter and killed about six of them. I think he's in prison now.

AND SO on the seventh hole Stu was throwing it. I told him that I'd read somewhere that the world record for throwing the ball for eighteen holes was ninety-three. "Jesus," I said. "We ought to both start throwing it."

When we got to the greens, he got down on his knees and shot the ball like a marble. He got a ten and a nine on the seventh and eighth holes.

As we were walking up to the ninth tee, he said in almost a whisper, "Let's go home, O.K.?"

"What?" I said. I was beating him for once. "You don't want to play the back nine?"

"No," he said. "No, let's just go to the house. Now. If you don't mind."

"All right," I said. "Sure. You're not sick, are you?"

"No," he said.

I put my driver back in the bag and started walking for the car.

About halfway down the fairway, he said, "Richard, promise me you'll never get married."

"What!" I said.

"Promise me."

"Sure," I said. "I hadn't planned on it. Why?"

"Because it doesn't work," he said. "I don't know. You see all these T.V. shows where everyone's happily married. Well, it's all a lot of bullshit. Don't ever buy that bullshit that it works, O.K.? Because it doesn't."

"I won't," I told him. "Trouble at home? You and Beck having some problems?"

"No," he said. "Yeah, sort of. Nothing I can't handle though. Nothing I can't handle."

On the next fairway, normal people were playing golf.

THAT NIGHT I picked Connie up at eight. We had been dating about two months. Nothing serious, just a nice, slow, no-obligations relationship. I don't care much for her. She's a nice girl and all, a blonde, on a good day she's probably a five on a scale of one to ten. She's not a barker. Don't get me wrong. Let's just say she's "sweet" looking. Personally, I prefer brunettes. But Connie doesn't give me any bullshit. That's what I like about her. She hardly says anything. So I'm sticking with her for the time being.

Connie had seen Stu over at my place, but she had never met Beck. I told her that Beck's real name was Rebecca, and that she'd probably better call her Rebecca at first. I told her that Beck taught at the high school–she was the girls' gym coach–and that she was probably the most beautiful brunette I had ever seen.

Connie asked me to stay close and not run off and leave her around people she didn't know very well.

When I turned onto Stu's street, I told her that this was the street I grew up on when we moved to the city, and that Stu's house was just two houses down from where Mama still lives. I told her how the old man died the week before I was to graduate from college and how, about six months later, Stu had bought his house to keep an eye on Mama.

I pulled into Mama's driveway and parked and told Connie that she'd better wait in the car until I saw if Mama was feeling O.K. Mama got "sick" just about every day and couldn't get to the phone, so it was good that Stu lived so close and could check in on her. If she was feeling like it, I was going to take her down to Stu's for some cake.

It was just about dark. The gaslight hadn't worked since the old man died. I picked up three morning papers from the lawn and got the mail from the box. Sometimes, I liked to see if any of it was still for me. The T.V. was blaring so loud I could hear every word before I opened the front door.

Mama was sprawled out on the couch with her mouth open, snoring. I turned the T.V. off. "Mama," I said. "Mama?" She didn't move. There was a cigarette still burning on the lip of the ashtray about to fall off onto the carpet. I didn't touch it. I figured that if it fell and the whole house burned to the ground with Mama in it, that somehow she'd be happy. I spread her afghan over her feet.

I wanted to look at my old room before I left. I hadn't seen it since I had moved out. It was at the end of the hall, next to Stu's old room. There was the fist hole at about eye level in my door. I hated coming back to that old room. I don't know what I expected, maybe for things to return to the way they had been before Stu moved out, before the old man died, before Mama got sick.

I had moved everything out when I left home, and Mama had taken down everything else, the pictures, the posters. She had even taken down the drapes.

I looked through the window and saw a young boy with a BB gun walking through the back yard. It was time to go.

Without thinking, I said, "Good-bye, Mama."

And she said, "You going?"

I turned around and said, "Yes, ma'am. I didn't mean to wake you." Her eyes were closed again, and she was snoring. I turned the T.V. on and walked out through the garage.

It was empty. Stu had moved all the old man's tools down to his garage, the table saws, the drill presses. He set them up exactly like the old man had them. He had his garage arranged exactly like the old man's used to be, a couple houses down. He even had the old man's sign, "Stuart Madden," nailed up over his workbench in just the right spot.

In a way, I think that Stu was trying to recapture the old man. Sometimes, when he gets pissed off and shouts at me, I'll jump just like I used to when the old man shouted at me. I can see the old man in him. And sometimes, I'll drive up in his driveway, and the garage door will be open, and he'll be slumped over his workbench, hammering or sawing on something, and for an instant, I'll think that he *is* Daddy and that I'd better hurry up and get in there and help him.

I turned off the garage light, closed and locked the door, and walked to the car. I told Connie, "Maybe you can meet her some other time."

"Is she sick?" Connie said.

"In a way," I said.

WHEN WE got to Stu's house, the garage light was on, and he was in there sawing. I knew that if he cared anything about seeing us he would have been inside. Besides, I wanted to see Beck first and see what was going on, so we walked up the sidewalk to the front door. I opened the door and said, "Knock, knock!"

Beck was in the kitchen. "Come on in," she said. "I'll be in there in a second." She walked around the bar, carrying the cake, and set it on the dining room table. She had different shades of icing on the sleeves of her pullover. She looked delicious.

"Hello, gorgeous," I said, and gave her a hug. "Beck, this is Connie. Connie, this is Beck." And before they could say their

"Nice to meet you's," I said, "What's old Stu doing in the garage?"

"He's on a little tirade," Beck said. "But it's his birthday." She smiled at Connie. "He's entitled to it."

"Sure," Connie said.

Beck pointed to the cake and shook her head. "Look what he did to my little golfer."

The cake was white with a putting green centered on the top of it. There was even a blue water hazard to the left of the green. On the green was a little man who looked like he was putting.

"That's adorable!" Connie said.

"I did it all myself," Beck said. "But look what he did."

I looked closer.

"I had to special order that little golfer from Houston," she said, "and a little while ago Stu walked through here with a pair of scissors or something and cut the guy's little putter off."

I could see the little guy on the green, but he didn't look much like a golfer. He looked more like one of those plastic army men I had when I was a kid, the one with the mine detector. This little guy was just standing there, holding something.

"I threw the little thing away," Beck said. "I thought it looked kind of disgusting."

"Well, I'll tell you what it looks like now," I said. "It looks like that little fellow's standing right out in the open, in front of God and everybody, and taking a piss right there on Stuart's birthday cake."

"Richard!" Beck said.

Connie bit her lip and shook her head.

I got a good chuckle out of it and said, "I'll go out and cheer up old Stubert."

"Good," Beck said.

"I'll go out and tell him some guy's in here taking a leak on his birthday cake." I gave Beck a big grin. She turned her head away from Connie and winked at me.

Stu was at his workbench with his back to me. He was using a hacksaw.

"Here's the birthday boy," I said. "Hey, not-so-big brother, Mama said to tell you she was sorry she couldn't . . ."

"Go back inside," he said. "I don't feel like talking to anyone." He had his golf bag leaning up against the workbench. He had something in the vise, and he was sawing.

"Why?" I said. "What are you working . . . What are you doing!" He had one of his new clubs, an iron, in the vise, and he was sawing it in half. I looked in the trash can, and he had already done two or three.

"Have you lost your fucking mind!" I said. "What's going on?"

"This," he said. The handle part of the club he was working on fell to the floor. He loosened the vise and gave me the other end. It was the seven iron. He pulled the six out of his bag and clamped it in the vise. He said, "This is what I think of Beck's little affair."

"What?" I said. I tried to sound surprised.

"Yeah, she's sleeping with someone."

"How do you know?" I said.

He stopped sawing. He turned around and looked at me. "I know," he said. "I don't know who it is yet, but I know she's doing it. You know, when we first got married, she told me that if I was to ever kiss another woman, I mean *really* kiss another woman, that she'd be able to tell. That works both ways, Sport. It works both ways."

"Come on," I said, "Beck wouldn't do that to you."

He started sawing again. "Yes, she would," he said. "You see, she hates me in a way. Just like you hate me, Richard."

"Let's just feel sorry for ourselves," I told him.

"Listen," he said, "if you're going to give me any of your bullshit, I don't want you out here!"

"O.K.," I said. "Sure. I get the picture." I opened the door.

"Hey, Scrotum!" he said. He still had his back to me. "I had a bad round today, and you beat me on what's been maybe the worst day of my life. Now, when you get home tonight, you be sure and celebrate."

I closed the door behind me. I could hear the girls talking. They were talking about school. Connie was studying to be a school teacher, and Beck was telling her about our school district. I put a smile on my face and walked into the dining room where they were drinking some of the birthday punch.

Beck stopped what she was saying and asked me, "Did you cheer him up?"

"Sort of," I said. I couldn't tell her. I knew there would be fireworks as soon as we left. I didn't particularly want to be around Beck and Connie in the same room so I asked her, "Where's little Stuart?"

"In his room," she said. "Don't get him all worked up."

The hallway was dark, and I could see the light on beneath his door. I knocked, and the light went off in the room.

"It's open," a voice said from inside. I opened the door and stepped in. "Close it behind you," the voice said. I was trying to locate him by the sound of his voice when a flashlight was shined in my face.

"Uncle Rick!" the voice said. "I didn't know it was you. Sometimes it gets pretty dangerous back here!"

"I bet it does," I said. "Where are the lights?"

"Behind you," he said.

I found the switch in the dark and flipped it. He turned the flashlight off. He was on the top bunk of Stu's old bunk bed. He had a football helmet on, a flashlight in one hand, and some kind of ray gun in the other.

"My god," I said. "It looks like you're ready for an attack."

"I am!" he said.

I stepped carefully over all the toys on the floor. "You know, Stuart, you really ought to clean this place up," I told him. "One of these days you're gonna get lost in here, and your mother's not going to be able to find you. Where are they?"

"I already set them up," he said.

"Good," I said. "Where's the gun?"

"I'll get it."

"Get that and get the tape."

He brought the tape and the BB gun that looked like a Winchester, and I started taping the flashlight to the left side of the gun barrel while he was opening the drapes and opening the window.

"You go first," he said and turned out the lights. He'd already taken the screen off when he'd crawled out the first time.

The windows in his room were full-length, so we had to get on our bellies to shoot. I cocked the Winchester and turned on the flashlight and surveyed the back yard. There were a dozen six-inch plastic army men situated at strategic places prepared to attack the Madden household. The way we played was that each of us took turns shooting, and whoever killed the most out of twelve won that round.

I located each soldier and shot the one closest to the house, a hand-grenade thrower, perhaps the most potentially dangerous. I handed him the gun.

"You know, Geek, you did a fine job setting up those men," I told him. "Now take that helmet off so you can see what you're doing!"

"You're the geek!" he said. "You even smell like a geek!"

"Shut up and shoot," I told him.

WE PLAYED about half an hour until I saw it was around ten and time for us to go. I helped him get the screen back on and close the window.

It had been a close game, and he had won, or he, at least, thought he had won.

I told him good night, closed his door, and walked back into the dining room. The girls were still talking, and they had already started on the cake.

I asked Beck, "Stu didn't blow out the candles?"

"Ha, ha," she said. "I thought we'd better go ahead without him. Besides, you don't ask a dragon to blow out candles."

I looked at Connie and said, "We'd better be going."

"You don't have to run off," Beck said.

I looked at her, pointed in the direction of the sawing, and nodded my head.

"You'll have to come back and see us," she said to Connie. "Hang on, and you can take some of this cake." She cut the cake and placed the pieces on two paper plates. She wrapped them and handed them to Connie.

We walked to the door. We said, "Good night."

Outside, I said, "I'll go say bye to Stu." I walked around to the side garage door. He was up to the woods now. He was on the three wood. I stepped inside and said, "Happy birthday, big brother."

"Yeah, *happy* birthday," was all he said.

I walked back around front. Connie was already sitting in the car with her door open. She had a paper plate in each hand. I waved at her and pointed to the front door. I wanted to tell Beck about Stuart. I wanted to warn her. I opened the door and leaned in and said, "Enjoyed it!"

She was clearing off the table. She looked at me, licked a light blue smear of icing from her finger, and said, "Tomorrow."

HOW FAR ARE WE
FROM THE WATER?

SADNESS IS fogging the back window, his tail wagging, his nose pressed against the pane.

"Shoo," she tells him. She takes off her sweater. "Shoo!" She is frowning. "We leave all these lights on?"

Both pole lamps on both sides of the love seat. The chandelier! The bare bulb above the kitchen sink. Even the back floodlights are on.

"We didn't, did we?" She looks behind her. "Ryne?" She walks back into the entry hall. "Where are you?" she says. The front door still open.

She pulls her key from the lock, steps onto the porch, and then she sees him, standing out in the yard, his hands in his jeans pockets. "Ryne?"

"You know what these are?" he says, nudging something in the tall grass with his boot.

She points. "I need to mow that."

"These," he says, kicking a large green bois d'arc ball onto the sidewalk.

"They come off that old tree," she says.

"They're called horse apples."

"Is that right," she says, walking slowly down the steps. "Ryne?"

A cold front blew through earlier in the evening. It has rained.

The bark on the bois d'arc is wet on the north side. The hanging Spanish moss in the live oak, soaked.

"Ryne," she says, "why don't you come on inside?" She reaches out her arm for him.

He looks up at her. He smiles. "You think it'd be all right?"

"Sure," she says. "Come on, now. We're letting all the bugs in."

He climbs the steps to the porch and walks slowly into the house.

She is standing out in the dark yard. Everything is too quiet now. There are no cicadas crying through the night. There are no bullfrogs from the bayou. No crickets. Is this it? she is thinking. Is this winter?

She is looking through the trees, down the long driveway to the levee. She is hoping to hear something in this silence. A car passing on the levee road. A small V of geese heading south. Anything.

"THIS IS really a nice place you got here," he says. He is standing in the den at the picture window.

"What's that?" she says, stepping out of the utility room. "Must have been every light in the house on."

"I was saying, You got a really nice place. It's even got a great backyard."

She just looks at him. "Yeah," she says. "It's got...grass and everything."

"This y'all's basset?"

Sadness waddles over to the back door. He looks at Ryne. He stops his tail. He looks at her, very disappointed.

"Get on," she says. She kicks at the panes in the door. "Get on away from there!"

"Can I get you something to drink?" she says, walking into the kitchen. She opens the refrigerator. "Let's see what we got in here," she says. "We got beer. Three beers. Lone Star."

"A beer'll be fine," he says.

"Some Cokes. Some Sprites. Got some old chicken in here. Want some chicken? Wine coolers. Got some wine. You like wine?"

He turns from the window. "I'll just take a beer," he says.

"White wine," she says. "Pretty cheap white wine I'm afraid." A bottle of champagne. She looks up out of the refrigerator. "What do you need?"

"A beer," he says.

"THANK YOU," he says.

"I'm going to have a little wine," she says, "if I can just get this bottle open."

"I see y'all got an airboat."

"What?" she says from the kitchen, opening and slamming drawers. "Where in the hell is that little thing?"

"The boat," he says. He points with his beer.

"The swamp boat," she says. "We had it out back by the garage, and somebody came by one night and stole the big airplane propeller type thing, so we had to move it inside the fence."

"It ain't much good without one," he says.

"You like wine?" she says. She walks into the den to the love seat.

"Sure," he says. "I haven't had much of it." He is looking at the garage. The side door is open. A light is on over the workbench. He can see a red vise, a welding machine, a small bateau. He says, "Don't know if I've ever had any wine."

"Do you know anything about it?"

"A little," he says, his back to her. "Not a whole lot. You know, people down here don't drink a lot of wine. Don't know if I know anybody that drinks wine."

"You do now," she says. She sits on the love seat. "Ryne?"

"How far are we from the water?"

"Ryne?"

He turns and looks at her. "Yes?" he says.

"Why don't you just come on over here and sit down?" she says. "I mean, you don't have to if you don't want to."

"You think?" he says.

"Sure," she says. She pats the seat beside her. "Here."

"I DON'T know what to make of this," she says, swirling the wine in her glass. "Want a sip?"

"Why not," he says and knocks down about a shot of it.

"What do you think?" she says.

He looks at the glass and frowns. "Not much of a bite," he says. "Tastes like old water. Flat water. Tastes like slow river water."

"I'm just learning," she says. "This probably isn't that good. I think you can run into a bad bottle every now and then." She lifts the glass and looks at it.

"It isn't really white, is it?"

"Pardon me?" she says.

"The wine," he says.

"No," she says. She just looks at him. "No, it isn't."

"But red wine is really red."

"Yes," she says. "It is."

"Why is that?"

SHE IS staring past him, out the window, into the yard.

"What is it?" he says. He turns in the love seat and follows her look. "What's the matter?"

Sadness is out there, deep in the yard, pointing toward the garage, his tail wagging.

"Nothing," she says. She turns, and her eyes catch the bootjack by the fireplace. "Thought I heard someone on the driveway."

"Want me to go check?"

"No," she says. "Wouldn't be anybody at this hour."

"So," he says. He sips his beer. "Where is he?"

"Who?"

"The man who takes that boat to the slough," he says. "If you don't mind my asking."

"No," she says. "Not at all." She says, "Gone."

"Gone?"

"We're divorced," she says.

"I'm sorry," he says. "I didn't know. I wasn't sure."

"Yeah," she says. "I would've told you. It's just that.... It's just that sometimes even *I* don't believe it."

"How long's it been?"

She is looking out the window again. "About a couple years," she says. "Somewhere in there." She is looking deep into the dark thicket, past the property line where even the floodlights will not go. "What is this? November? Two years, a couple months, and a week now. Something like that."

"I'm separated," he says, reading the label on his beer bottle.

"That's what you said," she says. "You said that you were."

"But we're getting a divorce," he says. "If that's what she wants. I mean, if that's what we decide on."

"It's hard," she says.

He looks at her. "Does it get any easier?"

"Not for a while," she tells him. "Not for a while." She shakes her head. "Listen," she says, "if you don't mind, could we change the subject?"

"I'm sorry," he says.

"No," she says. "It's all right."

"Really," he says, "we shouldn't be talking about this anyway. I shouldn't be."

"It just doesn't do any good, you know," she says. "It just doesn't." She catches herself in the middle of a yawn, covers her mouth with her hand. "Pardon me," she says.

"I'm keeping you up," he says.

"No," she says.

"You just run me off when you're ready."

"Don't worry," she says. She yawns again. "I'm sorry."

And then, he yawns.

They both laugh.

"It's catching," he says. "Have you ever thought about that?"

"What?"

"Yawning," he says. "Why we do it? Why *do* we yawn? How do we catch it from other people?"

"I don't know," she says. She is looking at the clock above the fireplace. It is getting late.

"Have you ever thought about why we don't catch yawns from TV?" he says. "I mean, they're real people in there, you know. And they yawn, and we don't. Why is that?"

"They probably aren't real yawns," she says. "They probably just acted-out yawns, the ones that aren't contagious."

"You think?" he says. "And even talking on the telephone. You can be just talking to somebody on the telephone, and you can't see their eyes start to water, and you can't see their mouth wide open. You can just *hear* them, and it makes you yawn."

"Is that right," she says.

"I don't know when," he says, "but I know for certain that I once caught a yawn from a dog."

"I need some more wine," she says. She stands and walks into the kitchen. "Can I get you another beer?"

"If you don't mind," he says, leaning back in the love seat. He is smiling.

He hears her laughing in the kitchen. "What?" he says.

"Nothing," she says. She carries a beer out to him, places it on the coffee table. She looks at him. She gives him a kind smile, shakes her head, and walks back into the kitchen.

"Was that stupid or what?" he says loud enough for her to hear him.

"What?" she says.

He picks up his beer. "Talking about yawning."

He hears her laughing. *No,* she says. She sticks her head around the corner. "No, I think it's...interesting. Let me get my wine."

He places his beer back on the coaster. He looks out the window and frowns. "I guess it was pretty stupid," he says to himself. "Who's that?"

"Who!" she says, walking quickly out of the kitchen.

The back door opens.

"That," he says.

"Mason!" she says.

But Mason has not stopped walking toward her. He has not even closed the back door. Sadness peeps his head around the corner. "Mason," she says, "Goddamnit!" She points at Ryne. "I've got...company."

Mason takes her by that hand and heads for the back of the house.

Ryne stands and looks confused.

"Excuse us," Mason tells him, pulling her gently into the back hallway.

"Goddamnit, Mason!" she says. She is walking behind him. She is being pulled along. She is not exactly resisting. "I have a guest in there!"

Without stopping, Mason points at the many pictures on the walls of the hallway. Family pictures. Her mother, her father. Donnie and Debbie. The nieces, the nephews. All smiling. "There we are," he says. "Happy."

"Don't do this," she says.

When they reach the dark bedroom, she stops, and he lets go of her hand and crawls onto the far side of the bed. He pats the comforter beside him. "Come here," he says.

"We ain't doing this again," she says. She stomps her foot. "Goddamnit!" She points through the wall. "I got a *date* in there!"

He reaches up with his finger and hooks one of her belt loops and pulls her slowly down onto the bed with him.

She sets her glass of wine on the night table. "This is it!" she says. "You hear me?"

He takes her softly by the shoulders and lays her down next to him.

"Just for a second, now," she says. "I got to get back."

He slides his left leg over her. He nestles up next to her. He rests his head on her breast. "Hold me," he whispers.

"Goddamnit, Mason."

He reaches up with his left hand and finds her face, her mouth. He carefully closes her lips with his fingers. "Shhh," he tells her. He places his finger on her lips. "Shhh," he says.

The house is quiet. She is listening for Ryne. She is listening for the sound of the front door opening, listening for the sound of his truck starting, the sound of his tires on the oyster-shell driveway.

"Tell me," he says.

"What?" she says.

"Tell me everything's gonna be all right."

She places her hand on the side of his face. "Mason," she whispers.

"Tell me."

"Everything's gonna be all right," she says.

She feels something large land at their feet. "Did you leave the door open?" she says. "Did you let the dog in?" She lifts her head and looks down, and there he is, in silhouette, Ryne, slumped over, sitting at the foot of the bed.

"Tell me," he says.

CHOCOLATE BAY

THERE IS a full moon, but we cannot see it. It is up above the trees, hidden by the branches.

Both of us have our torches going. I have my knife out.

Do you know where we are?

If you should lose me...

Sort of, she says.

... head east through the forest...

I look at my compass. We are heading east.

The trees here, tall, gaunt, died some time ago. They stand—without leaves, without bark—bleached bone white in the moonlight.

My torch is failing. I shake it, stare into its flickering light, and when I look up again, temporarily blinded, she is gone.

... until you find the road.

There is a rusty, sagging barbed wire fence with delicious decorations—bright green spoons, pink plastic worms, empty hooks.

Every now and then, I catch a faint glimpse of her torch through the trees.

She has let her hair down by now, black as this night, long to the waist, flowing out straight behind her like a mane.

A break in the trees, a long clearing, a pass—the road.

Follow it north, up and over the hill...

Up above, flocks of sacalait head south.

Even here, on this scar in the wood, a drowned moon lights the road up the rise.

At the top of the hill, nipple-deep, her white bikini top floats, empty, unclasped, the large cups filled with water.

Carefully, I fold cup into cup, press them to my cheek—are they still warm—look *down into the valley, and I will be waiting*.

I swam around in front of her, and with my free hand I spelled out, Air time.

Soon, she told me.

A large catfish darted past us and disappeared into the trees.

I was shaking my head, drawing my forefinger across my throat.

THERE ARE roads at the bottom of the lake. There is an old town. The houses still standing, no roofs.

Looking down into this valley just before dawn is like looking down into a village, no lights on, when everyone is asleep.

I tuck her top into my swimsuit and hurry after her. Swimming quickly down the hill, I find the next thermocline.

THERE ARE layers of water in a freshwater lake, layers of consistent temperature. And as you sink down deeper in the water, these thermoclines get colder.

You can be swimming along horizontally and dip just your fingers into the lower layer and feel the chill. Sometimes, they are six feet thick. Sometimes, ten, twelve.

I can imagine her now, hurrying down this hill, falling into this colder water, topless, nipples hard, goose pimples on her naked shoulders.

ON THE road south of town, someone was leaving. There is an old car, its driver's door open, its hood up.

You can stand at the end of the main street and watch large fish swim from the windows of the houses on one side of the street into the windows on the other side.

All the front doors are open as if everyone left late one night when a big rain came.

It is a dark town always, sometimes lighter in the day.

Clouds of bream pass the moon.

I am slamming the butt of my torch into the palm of my hand, and when it shines it catches the white bottom of her bikini, untied, waist-deep in the water, some thirty feet ahead of me right in the middle of Main Street.

And then so suddenly—do you know the feeling? You are wading through weeds in a field, hunting. It is a bright day, no clouds. Or maybe you are not hunting, do not have a gun. Maybe you are looking for something lost in this ocean of yellow when it hits you—a hawk, a buzzard, a wide-winged bird flying overhead, high above, dragging its shadow across the field.

You have not seen the bird, do not know it is there, but it is a shiver you feel as the shadow passes, blocks the sun for an instant, takes with its talons a second of your breath, and you duck to one side, flinch a little.

And then so suddenly—it is like that day in the field—flinching, ducking from something not seen, feeling something large overhead pass the moon, I lose my footing, fall backwards, catch with the beam of my torch—her, naked, large breasted, subtle wings of hair down the insides of her thighs.

I am lying on my tank like a turtle on its back, trying to get to my feet, but she is gone just as quickly, her legs pumping hard, she disappears over a house on the other side of the street.

Seven hundred pounds of air. In around twenty minutes, I will have to leave this town.

There is a two-story house at the end of the main street. A tall pale woman stands on the upstairs verandah. She beckons me. I can see her in the moonlight.

I grab my swimsuit on both sides and jerk it down to my knees, down to my ankles, falling on my bottom on the bottom of the lake. I stab the knife into the street beside me.

Trying to take a swimsuit off over scuba fins is like trying to take jeans off over boots. It won't go, so I'm standing now, hobbling about in the middle of Main Street, stomping around like I'm trying to pull my feet out of a tar road.

Fifteen minutes.

So I take the knife out of the ground and cut the crotch out of the swimsuit, cut it off my fins. I slip out of the straps of my backpack and push the tank behind me so hard it rips the regulator out of my mouth.

Stupid, I tell myself and swim back for it, the hose wriggling, bleeding bubbles.

I purge the regulator of water, take the tank out of the backpack, take it by the neck, tear my fins off, ditch my weight belt, and hurry for her. But now, without the weight belt, I am too light to run down the street. Now, without the fins, it is like swimming without feet.

There is a rusty umbrella's skeleton hiding behind the front door. There is no answer, so I push it open and with the tank under my arm swim up the stairs. Scattered up the steps, her fins, her bootees, her backpack on the landing.

The master bedroom has a large picture window that looks out over the town. She has stood her torch on its end in the corner. She is standing at the window, wearing a mask, that is all. She is floating some three inches from the floor, touching herself gently with both hands. Her eyes closed. Her breasts, which have already begun to sag slightly, float now at just the right height. Her long hair writhes in this still water. Her tank suspended above her like an emptying idea.

She opens her eyes, sees me, stops that gentle rubbing just long enough to spell with her right hand, Hurry.

TEN MINUTES, and I am pulling her to me hard, weightless, her legs locked behind me, and when I open my eyes, we are some ten feet above the bedroom, ten feet above the house, drifting out over Main Street, turning ever so slowly end over end.

No STORMS disturb this street, this drowned town.

It is almost dawn, and I can see the beam of her torch shining out of that bedroom, straight up out of the lake where it catches the bottom of a lone boat.

Maybe there is an elderly couple in the boat, fishing at just dawn. They have gotten up too early on this morning, and maybe the old woman nods off occasionally, her rod tip dipping into the water. The fish have long since stolen her bait.

The old man sits in the back of the boat. He has not been fishing for so long that he is trying to remember this lake, clouded now in mist, trying to remember the rules like where to hook the minnows so that they will not die, like how to keep the line taut so that he can feel the first nibbles, whether to go to lures and when.

His hands are cold, so he takes turns keeping one in the pocket of his jacket.

Yes, he hooked the minnow too shallow on the lips. Yes, he

lost the bait on his first cast, slung it far into the mist, so that it swims quickly now, frightened, for the deep water.

He does not know this, and in a while he will wonder why he has had no bites. But, for now, he is watching bubbles come to the surface on both sides of his boat. He is listening to the sounds these bubbles release as they burst on the surface of the water–animal sounds, growling noises, screams, purrs–so that he wants to lean and whisper to his wife, her back to him, "Listen." But he is frightened. He does not move.

TWO

WE RENTED the house in Chocolate Bay the day before we were married. There is a peninsula, a crescent moon, which curves out into the water some half mile. We rented the house at the tip of the moon because it was cheaper there.

"This all used to be a real show place," Mr. Burnet told us. "The country club section of town. All the oil executives lived out here." He was wearing a white starched shirt, khaki pants. He was probably a defensive lineman fifty years ago, but now he had the belly. He had his hands in his pockets.

It was low tide, and we were standing in the backyard, looking out over the water. We could see the mainland, the empty houses all along the far shore. They, too, were outside the levee. Some of them were out in the bay. Some fifty yards out. Some one hundred yards.

"You understand," Mr. Burnet said, "we have a little problem with subsidence out here."

"We understand."

"That's why the rent's so low," he said. "Subsided some nine feet since the twenties." He smiled at us. "The refineries up the

Channel are to blame. They keep pumping out the ground water. We keep sinking."

"Perfect," I told him. "We just want to be off away from everybody else."

He laughed. "Y'all be that out here." The smile left his face. "Y'all be about the only ones left out here now." He pointed across the bay. "Maybe there's a family or two living over in those houses.

"Course, you know," he said, moving his hand from our house up the road around the moon to the mainland, "at high tide, you'll be cut off."

"Good," I told him.

"Unless y'all have any questions," he said, "I'd better get on back to Mama."

Allison said, "You didn't leave her in the car?"

He started walking. "Oh, it's all right," he said. "She's just old is all. Tired." He was smiling again. "Had to bring her along. This used to be her house, you know."

When we got around front, the car was empty, the passenger door open.

"Mama?" Mr. Burnet said.

Maybe she had walked out back looking for us. Or maybe she was inspecting the azaleas around the house, her azaleas.

"There she is!" Mr. Burnet said, and we all walked out to get her. She was standing, her back to us, where the road disappeared under the bay. She had left her shoes on the road, and she was just standing there, ankle-deep, about twenty feet out in the water.

"Mama?" Mr. Burnet said. He picked up her shoes, walked out and put his arm around her. Salt water in his wingtips.

She was wearing a pale peach duster, faded from too many

washings. She did not say hello. Mr. Burnet walked her to the passenger side and seated her politely like a date.

He hurried around the rear of the old Cadillac and opened his door. Mrs. Burnet was staring straight ahead. He rolled his window down. "And if," he said, climbing into the car, "if there's so much as a whisper of a storm in the Gulf..." He closed the door and looked out at us. "Get out." He started the engine. "Get out quick."

We watched the slow car follow the road around the peninsula.

Allison looked at the house, at the large live oak stretching far and low over the lawn. She looked at me. "Is this the place?" she said. "Is it what you want?"

I cupped my hands around her face, pulled her to me, kissed her, and said, "It's what I *need.*"

WE RENTED the house in Chocolate Bay even though it needed some work. *It was perfect.* Seven miles from town. No neighbors, no visitors, no telephone calls.

I started by raking the yard carefully to find any storm debris Burnet might have missed, scraps of driftwood, strips of shingles, a pair of baby shoes hiding in the grass—a tight pair of pantyhose will ruin a good lawn mower—things I didn't want picked up and thrown by the blade. I mowed the front yard to the road, the backyard to the brown line.

I shoveled the inch or so of storm silt off the driveway, washed it down with the hose, let it dry, swept it clean.

Burnet had a new cyclone fence installed where the old one had been, the back gate well beyond where the salt water had already killed the St. Augustine.

The pier was the first thing to go when the tide came in, so I had to wade out periodically and scrape the barnacles, scrub the algae, so it would stay safe enough to walk out on.

I drove into town and bought a swing set at Western Auto. I brought it home and put it together and placed it in the backyard just inside the brown line.

Allison scrubbed out the bathrooms, the sinks, the commodes—up until about a month after we had moved in, we still had tiny hermit crabs scurry up from the drains in the bathtubs.

She mopped the terrazzo in the entry hall, in the kitchen. She sponged out each cabinet and called me in from working outside to show me the stiff silver-dollar-sized shad trapped in the lower drawers as the waters receded.

She had already decided that the front bedroom would be the nursery, and she worked especially hard in there, laying new padding, new carpet, washing the baseboards.

She repainted the entire room a light aqua, and because we lived on the bay, she painted the bottom half a midnight blue. On the aqua, she painted pelicans sitting on posts in the water, seagulls skirting a southeast breeze. Down below, she painted smiling sea horses, happy fishes, dancing dolphins.

CHOCOLATE BAY took some getting used to. We had to learn to synchronize ourselves with the tides. We had to keep track of them on the radio.

Allison learned to hurry home from the hospital—to run her errands—when the tide was out, so she could cross the low road from mainland to peninsula.

If she miscalculated the time, she would stop the car up on the levee by the pump station, honk and wave at me across the water, and then drive back into town to her mother's with the groceries, the milk, the biscuits, the butter, and bacon.

Some Sunday evenings, after working hard around the house, we would sit in the backyard in chaise longues and have a toddy or two and watch it get dark on the water.

We would just sit there and watch the tide come in, watch it slowly take the pier, sneak through the cyclone, creep into our yard.

We watched the large ships far in the distance come up the Channel.

We watched the other couple across the bay come home in the evenings, park their car on the levee road, and take the boat out to their house.

We watched them park their car at dusk, watched them carry groceries down the pier to the boathouse. She would load the sacks into the boat. He would start the motor, which roared across the still bay. And whatever we were doing, wherever we were in the house or the yard, we would say, "They're home."

Sometimes, we would wave at them across the water, and Allison would look at me and say, "We aren't the only idiots in the world."

They would dock the boat at the back porch and walk into the dark house. First, we would see the kitchen light—she, unloading groceries. Then, the bathroom light—maybe he had a beer on the way home from the store. And finally, the house dark again, a pale blue glow from the upstairs bedroom late into the night.

Most of the houses out here are mere shells of the once homes. We rented the last house on the lee side because somehow it had weathered the last hurricane.

Years ago, the corps of engineers raised the road on the peninsula so that it became a levee of sorts, a windbreak. The row of large live oak all along the road must have broken some of the wind.

I could tell where Burnet had come along and replaced windows, repainted doors, reshingled the entire roof.

But the houses on the harm side of the peninsula, unprotected as they were, caught the bare brunt of the last storm.

Directly across the road—some fifty yards from front door to front door—the house is a skeleton. The roof is intact in most places, but what is odd about these houses is that they have no walls. There is no brick—just the two-by-four frames. I can stand on the road and look through the house to the water. There is no sheetrock, no paneling. What did this? A large piece of driftwood used by a wild sea as a battering ram? Several pieces? An entire roiling sea of wood?

The front lawn is knee-deep in St. Augustine. Six-foot sweetgum saplings grow throughout the yard. The driveway, the sidewalk, grown over. Nature is taking this place back.

I step through the picture window into the house, and two calico kittens dart through the den. I have to be careful in these houses in the late afternoons, barefooted, the rusty nails, the broken glass. The floor is littered with once soggy sheetrock, contorted coat hangers, credit card receipts, socks, tattered strips of carpet covered with a fine layer of silt.

In the hallway, I find a new pair of blue jeans. I pick them up, shake the dried mud off of them. A boy's? Not quite two feet long. How old was he? Six, seven? Kindergarten, first grade?

Poison ivy carpets the master bedroom. Birds nest in the medicine cabinet.

I walk through a wall and find old records strewn about the

floor, 45s. Some stepped on, broken. "Bad Moon Rising" by Creedence Clearwater Revival. Some Skynyrd. ZZ Top.

Stacks of comic books in the closet.

A naked doll without a head sits on the windowsill and looks out over the bay.

In the far corner of the room, someone swept the concrete clean. I kneel here and find the scattered letters of an old Scrabble set. Most of the wooden squares dumped in a pile, but off to one side, five of them, S T O R M .

THIS EVENING, I am out fishing off the pier. Allison is sitting in her chaise longue. I spent most of the afternoon working on the tide. I purchased twenty broomsticks and painted them white and painted black marks on them in inches.

Our backyard is ninety feet deep, some sixty wide, so I started with the back fence and hammered in the markers every three feet, coming up the cyclone, ten on each side of the yard. This is so I can monitor the tide, measure the changes, how far it comes into our yard, how some days are deeper than others. We rented the house in Chocolate Bay so I could be near the water, away from the city, close to the stars.

Sometimes, I leave the back gate open in the late afternoons when the tide is coming in. Already, it covers half the lawn.

I drove into town to the hardware store and bought about one hundred and fifty feet of rope. I tied one end to the gate, ran the rope through the loops at the top of the cyclone, up one side of the fence to the house.

And late at night, I turn on the rear floodlights, open the back door, and pull the rope which closes the gate down by the pier.

Then I take my seine and wade out deep into the yard, hoping for cut bait for the next day of fishing, hoping for hardhead, sheepshead, croaker.

THIS EVENING, I am fishing off the pier, knee-deep in the water. Usually, I wade on out about one hundred yards into the bay where it is still only nipple-deep. I wade out there and cast as far as I can, trying for the shoals. But some afternoons, the tide catches me.

I have the stringer tied to the light pole at the end of the pier, far enough away from me in case a shark comes up. I pull it out of the water and wave it at her, a nice-sized speckled trout.

She does not wave back.

There are trees at the tip of the moon on both sides where the road disappears under the bay. Most of them are dead now—without leaves—killed by the salt water. At night, big black hulking birds sleep in their branches.

Allison is just sitting there, drinking a glass of wine, staring out over the water. I walk up to her, grab a beer out of the ice chest, and plop down into my chair.

"I don't like it out here," she says. She is not leaning back in her chaise longue. She is sitting up, her back straight, her feet on the ground. "I don't," she says. "I don't like it."

"Isn't it wonderful?"

"Not anymore."

A large oil tanker is coming up the Channel on the far side of the bay.

"It's spooky out here," she says. "By ourselves. Cut off."

I reach over and give her a loud kiss on the cheek.

She flinches. "No, I mean it," she says. "I'm serious. None of my friends will come and see me. They drive out here, and they're afraid to leave the levee."

The wake from the tanker pushes the bay to our chairs. She

jerks her feet up. "I hate this," she says. She's thinking, Salt water ruins Reeboks. "You hear me? I hate it."

"I know."

All of the grass is gone outside the fence. The brown line is about two feet closer to the house now. At high tide, the swing set stands some foot out in the bay.

"This is no place to raise a family," she says finally.

"Allison," I say. "We're not going to be out here *that* long."

"I don't know, Drew," she says. She looks at me. "I can see you staying out here forever. I can see you staying out here long after the bay has swallowed this whole backyard, this whole house. It will, you know," she says. "Sooner or later, it will. I can see you living up on the roof with your lantern, your fishing pole, and your goddamn goofy measuring sticks."

I catch myself looking up at the roof, thinking about where it would be level enough to stretch out a sleeping bag, where I could secure things, tie them down so they wouldn't roll off into the water—ice chests, canned goods, toilet paper. "No," I tell her. "No way."

"This is no place for this baby," she says. "No place for him to grow up."

"Come on," I tell her. "Just think what we could teach him, about things nobody knows anymore, about the water, the fish—*nature.*"

"What *you* could teach him."

"You can teach him whatever you want," I tell her. It is dark now, and I can barely see the small ferry crossing at Lynchburg. "God, I would've loved to have grown up out here, some place like this."

"No," she says in almost a whisper.

"What about all the work we've done?" I ask her. "The yard, the house, the nursery?"

"I don't want my baby's toys scattered across a muddy backyard. Look at us," she says. "We live in the fucking bay!"

"Allison," I say.

"Listen," she says. "I've done this. I've done this for you. I've moved out here, cleaned this place up for nothing—just to have the bay take it back whenever it wants to. I've helped you move furniture at a too-high tide. I've had to replace carpet, carry crabs out of my own kitchen.

"I'm tired of water in my house," she says. Her wine glass is empty. "I don't want my baby crawling around on a floor...No telling what's in that bay water!"

"Allison."

"Listen to me," she says. "I've done all this for you. I've lived out here for more than a year. Now it's your turn. When the baby's born, we're moving into town, or *I'm* moving into town. I'll stay with Mama if I have to."

I stand and walk back out into the yard, wade through the gate onto the pier, knee-deep in the water. I cast two shrimp far out over the bay, hoping for a nice redfish.

She has walked up to the house. She is standing at the back door, saying something to me, but I pretend I cannot hear her. She is saying, "I mean it."

HALFWAY AROUND the crescent moon, a battered house backs up to the bay. At high tide, the patio is underwater.

In the garage, on what is left of the sheetrock, someone spray painted, "Posted: Keep out!" For looters? For someone like me?

There is a line of silt and dead grass stuck to the walls three inches from the ceiling—the watermark. How long does the bay stay up after a storm?

The water heater knocked through the wall into the kitchen. The washing machine lies on its side in the den.

The entire back wall of this home is missing. The bay licks at the lip of the foundation. Some beast crept up from the deep water late one night and took in its maw the back side of this house.

In the den, a massive stone fireplace takes up a complete wall. Above the mantel, someone painted, "Don't cry."

A rusty fan without any blades hangs from the ceiling.

The study is ankle-deep in books. I sit on a love seat which looks like it has been dipped in chocolate. I go through the books one by one.

At the bottom of the pile, I find a photo album, the pages stuck together. I pull them apart carefully. A small child stands at the end of a pier. A young girl holding a present. A mother and a father with their arms around a young woman. Cap and gown. Wedding pictures. Why were these left behind?

Wisteria vines pour over the windowsill.

One at a time, I remove the pictures from the pages. I carry the photograph of the young girl back into the den. It was taken here, in front of a fire at Christmas. Red stockings hang behind her. The young girl is smiling, missing teeth, her fingers already under the bow. I place the photograph on the mantelpiece.

In the graduation picture, she is standing—very proud—on the front porch by the wooden plaque that reads, "The Ferrells." I place the picture in the mailbox filled with leaves.

The photograph of the three of them was taken in the kitchen. They are standing in front of a window with lace curtains. The mother and the father are laughing, slightly overweight. The young woman appears confused, frowning, pointing at the camera. Who took this picture? A grandmother? The young woman's fiancé? I place them carefully on the windowsill so that she is pointing now—concerned—out over the water.

"You GET some old scrap," I tell him, "like this chicken neck, and you tie your kite string to it. You need a weight too, or some people just tie a rock near the bait so that it will sink to the bottom." I toss it off into the water.

"Don't be like your mother and forget to tie the other end to the pier," I say. "And then you wait."

"Do you see how loose the line is? This is like fishing, but instead of watching a cork, you watch the line."

"Look, something's already taken it," I tell him. "Now, if you are fishing, and something takes the bait, you set the hook hard, right? But, you see, here you don't have a hook." I get down on my hands and knees on the pier. I take the line gingerly with both forefingers, one behind the other. "Here," I say, "all you have is the line and the bait—and you have their hunger."

I reach behind me and grab the net on the long pole. This is all it takes for Robin to go crazy. He is sitting in his walker, grinning, too tiny to talk, clapping his hands. Already, he knows that something is going to happen.

"This is the important part," I tell him. "You have to lure him to the surface slowly. If you so much as slightly jerk the line, he'll let go of the bait, and he's gone."

I am holding the line in one hand, the net in the other. I look at him. "Are you listening?"

Robin is resting his chin on the tray of his walker. He is staring intently at the line.

"You don't have to pull him completely out of the water. That's the mistake most people make. He ain't gonna let you do that anyway. He's not going to allow himself to be taken out of his element.

"Pay attention," I tell him. "You want to wait until you can first barely see him shallow in the water—can you see him? You can almost always see the chicken first because it's whiter, but he's on it—you can feel him. Wait until then to ease the net beneath the surface *behind* him because that's the direction he'll run."

Robin is frowning, taking all this in.

"Understand, you don't want to try to capture him. You don't want to try to scoop him up in the net. No. Because of the refraction, you'll miss him anyway. You'll just spook him. What you want to do is tease him to the surface with the bait and then wait with the net behind him.

"There he is, probably feeling himself pulled, probably already tasting the chicken, he sees the surface coming, he sees a man and a boy on a pier, he is connected to them by a white cotton line. The chicken is moist, enough to feed him for three days, but he is getting close to the surface, really too close now, something is wrong—he runs!" I lift the large blue crab from the water.

Robin squeals with delight, stomping his little feet.

I arc the net over him on my way to the ice chest, spraying salt water on his face. He loves it.

I hear a horn honking across the bay. "Look!" I tell him, pointing over the water. "It's your mother. Wave!" She has just passed the pump station, pulled off the levee road onto the peninsula.

I take the crab out of the net and show it to him.

Robin is giggling, reaching for it, opening and closing his hands quickly.

The crab is opening and closing its claws.

"You want to hold this crab?" I ask him.

Robin strains against the walker, trying to push himself closer, but he can't. I have wedged the front rollers into the cracks of the pier, in between the boards.

"Are you crazy!" I say. "This old crab would snip off every one of them fingers."

I open the ice chest and drop the crab in. It lands with its claws in the air, scuttles back into a corner.

"What are you doing with that baby on the pier!" she says, walking quickly down the yard. White dress, white shoes.

I look at Robin. "We're in trouble," I tell him. "Dinner, dear!"

"Drew!" she says. She walks up on the pier and lifts him out of his walker. "Now, goddamnit!"

"Me and him are quite a team," I tell her. "Look what we caught for you." I lift the ice chest. "For tonight."

"We've talked about keeping him away from the water!" she says.

"I was minding my own business," I tell her, "and he comes strolling on out here following me." I walk over and tickle him. "You're worse than a dog, you know that?"

Robin laughs. He is softly hitting his mother's nose with the palm of his hand like he wants a little horn to go off.

"I'm serious," she says. "What if—when he learns to walk—he gets away from us and comes out on this pier alone? He's already fascinated with the water. He's going to break loose every chance he gets and head out here!"

"What do you want me to do?" I ask her. "Make him *afraid* of the water? Scare him with it? Besides, we got a goddamn fence! When he learns to walk, we'll keep the gate closed. Hell, I'll even lock it!"

She shakes her head. "We're not going to be out here that long," she says. She is looking at Robin, touching him on the side of his face. She says something else, but it is like she is speaking only to him. She says, "We're not."

I pour the ice chest onto the pier. The crab is ready for us, claws in the air.

"Shoo," I tell it. "Go away." I hear the car start around in front of the house. I hear it back down the drive.

The crab backs over the edge and plops into the water.

The sun has gone down, and I can imagine her car following the moon around to the mainland. I can see the beams from her headlights catch one by one the dark, deserted houses on the far side of the bay.

DALLAS IS playing Miami on *Monday Night Football.* Allison has driven into town to a baby shower for one of her friends. Robin and I are sitting in the den, watching the game.

At this time of year, in the fall, the wind shifts from the southeast, from the Gulf, to the northwest. The nights are cooler, less humid, so we leave the windows open. There is a nice breeze coming in from the bay. The back door is open.

It's halftime, and I'm in the bathroom, thinking, The tide is out. She'll have no trouble getting home.

Robin sits quietly in his mother's chair and watches me watch the game. When the Cowboys score or intercept a pass and I jump up and down, he jumps up and down. Sometimes, we dance together. Sometimes, I piggyback him, screaming, out the front door to the road and back.

When White is sacked, when he fumbles the ball, I turn my head slowly and look at Robin. He has not been watching the television. He has been watching me. He knows that something bad has happened, so he frowns, shakes his head from side to side, very disappointed.

I hurry down the hall and into the kitchen for a beer so I won't miss the kickoff, but when I fall into my chair, turn to tickle him, he is gone.

"Robin?" I say. He is hiding. I look behind my chair, behind the couch. Maybe he went to the bathroom. "Hey," I say down the hallway. The light is off. Maybe he followed me into the kitchen for some cookies. "Robin?"

I turn the television down, and then I hear it—a cry, a loud bleating. I look through the back door, and the gate is open. "Robin!" I shout and sprint down the yard.

I stop at the gate, and there he is, standing at the end of the pier, his back to me, his arms stretched out wide on both sides.

The bleating, the strange laughter, is coming from the bay. There is motion in the water at the end of the pier.

"Robin?" I whisper, tiptoeing up behind him. "Sweetheart, what is it?" and when my eyes adjust to the darkness, I see them, dolphins, maybe three or four of them.

Robin is smiling.

When the dolphins see that I am there, they slowly stand in the bay and swim away from us, crying as they go, back to the deep water.

THREE

IN THE afternoons now, I sit in the backyard in my chaise longue and watch it get dark on the water. I watch the tide come in, watch it take the pier, swallow it.

I sit and watch all this, staring at the water. I cannot see it move as it slowly sneaks toward me, up past where I am sitting, almost to the house now. At night, the ice chest tied to my armrest floats between the two chairs.

But about this time in the afternoons, when the sun is going down, she comes. She parks her car on the levee road by the pump station, and she looks at me. I look back. We are just sitting there, watching each other across the water.

For some thirty or so minutes she sits there, her face pointed at me. Maybe her eyes are closed. I can't tell from this distance. It doesn't matter.

She just sits there and looks at me. Maybe our eyes meet over the water. We have that much. Then she starts her car and drives away.

We are getting somewhere.

She doesn't wave. She doesn't honk her horn. She just starts her car, turns her face from me, and drives away.

IF I can understand the tide, I can understand what has happened.

I chart it every afternoon, measure it day by day, high, low, when it comes in, when it leaves, how deep it gets at the back of the yard, how far it comes up the lawn.

I wade out into the yard, through the gate, onto the pier. I wade out and make measurements. I take notes on my clipboard:

At the end of the pier: 25¼ inches.

At the alpha markers, just inside the back fence: 24½ inches.

At the epsilon, five markers in: 22.

The kappa, thirty feet into the yard: 19¼.

The bay is some sixteen inches closer than when we moved in.

I close the gate behind me and walk up to the house to change pants, thinking, It will be four years Sunday. Ascertain month-by-month variations in the depths of the tides for a forty-eight-month period. How quickly are we sinking? How much deeper was December? At high tide, the bay is x inches higher from April to

May? How does this work? Plot average monthly tidal variations for first year, for second year...

I will figure it out over a beer—study the results and predict the hunger of the tide for the next twelve months (a bay at my back steps?), the next sixty (how soon will I have to move?)—but when I open the door, the house is empty. The furniture, gone.

The couch, her chair, my chair, missing. The television. The dining room set. Diplomas. Pictures on the wall.

Robin's room, vacant.

They left the bed in the bedroom, some linens in the bathroom.

In the kitchen, they left a few dishes, some cooking utensils—enough to survive with.

I open the refrigerator, take two six-packs, fill the ice chest. I grab my sleeping bag from the hall closet and head out.

Maybe I did hear vehicles pull up to the front of the house. Maybe I heard the hushed voices.

IN THE evenings now, I head out around the moon to the Ferrells' for a winter night by a fire.

I have cleared their den of all the debris, raked it out of the house, swept the foundation. I spent all one afternoon cleaning the fireplace.

There is no shortage of firewood on the peninsula, so some evenings after a good dinner, I carry my ice chest, my sleeping bag, make myself a nice fire, stretch out on the floor of the den and sleep.

And sometimes, in the middle of the night, when the fire has died down, I wake and watch the stars.

Most of the roof is missing. I can look up through the ceiling and see the sky. Only the roof rafters and ceiling joists remain–darker than the night–a perfect grid for studying the stars.

I have driven into town to the library and checked out books on the heavens, the constellations. I am studying them, learning their names.

So late at night, in the early mornings, I lie there on a dark peninsula in a house with no roof and watch Orion, the hunter, and at his heel Canis Major chases Lepus, the hare, toward the river Eridanus.

THIS IS what I told her. There is a time in the evening between light and dark when everything is without color. There is a time when the tide comes in ever so slowly, when the water rises until that exact moment when the surface is even with the top of the pier, when the pier looks like a bridge slightly submerged in the middle or an unfinished one leading off into the deep water. I am certain this is when it happened.

I told her that he was a child of the water, that he was conceived there, that he walked out on the pier to cross that bridge and left us. Maybe the dolphins caught him, one under each arm, and carried him out into Chocolate Bay.

I WAKE to the sound of someone whispering through the night. There is a full moon. I unzip my sleeping bag, sit up, and listen. I can hear someone whispering far away.

I find myself walking up the road, stopping at each house along the way, listening in the front door–not here.

I can hear the same message over and over again. I can make out consonants in the dark, vowels sometimes from this distance.

There is a two-story house at the end of the road. I am heading for it, moving so slowly, my entire body wading. The front door is open.

The voice is becoming more and more recognizable. I can hear it—letter by letter, word by word—"If you should lose me..."

I climb the stairs too easily and get the feeling I should not be here, I should not have come, I should go back down the peninsula to the house with no roof and a fire. It is another calling—to return—so I must hold on to the banister.

I hear someone giggling from down at the end of the hallway. I steady myself with the walls on both sides. I walk slowly through the doorway into the master bedroom, and there he is, sitting in the corner, naked, laughing, baby bream kissing the tips of his fingers, a large catfish curled at his feet.

I reach out to take him in my arms, to hold him to me closely, but even now I am leaving, rising up out of the bedroom, up out of the house.

If I could call his name, if he could only hear it, but when I open my mouth only bubbles come out, floating far above the house, rising high into the sky, until my head breaks the surface, my face wet, I open my eyes.

WESTERNS

MY FAMILY deals in motion. My old man's great grandfather sold shoes. My great grandfather sold horses and then wagons and carriages. My grandfather and my old man, automobiles. And I think that it's this inherited impulse to move that has made it so difficult for me to sit still in college classrooms, taking notes for hours.

This is my fourth state university. It's midterm, spring semester. I'm passing. I have just received a B on a medieval history exam. I am learning the difference between the active and the contemplative. I am concentrating on the contemplative.

The telephone rings. It is the old lady. "It's your father," she says. "He's had a stroke. Not a bad one, though. How's school?" She is trying to keep from crying. "Don't you worry about him," she says. "He's going to be all right." Then a silence. Then, "Please come home."

THE BEAUMONT U-Haul man wants to demonstrate how to hook the trailer to my truck. I tell him, no, that I've had plenty of experience.

I pack all my things. I say good-bye to everyone in the dorm. I tell them I'll be back in a week. I won't make it back. I know that. Someone will have to run the old man's business until he gets on his feet. He has a used car lot. Shawn is too young. This all works out too well for the old man. Me and the kid working at the lot together. Me, out of school.

I haven't been home since Christmas when I was having trouble with my Oldsmobile. The transmission, I think. Only the old man knew why I was really home for the holidays. He loaned me a nice Chevrolet truck. I knew my old car wasn't nice enough to be on his front line, but I left it with him anyway, ate Christmas dinner, and drove the nice truck back to Beaumont.

He had my Oldsmobile fixed and kept it on the back lot all spring and had Wylie wash it every now and then.

"Don't upset him," the nurse whispers. "He needs his rest."

"Sure," I tell her.

He has his eyes closed. On one night table, there are pots of plants and flowers. On the other, his Stetson, upside down.

"Daddy?" I say.

"Shawn?" he says.

"No sir. It's me."

He opens his eyes. "Hey," he says. He looks and sounds very tired. "Why aren't you at school?"

"I came home for a little visit."

He pushes a button in a small box resting on the sheet next to his hand. The head portion of the bed rises until he's in a sitting position. "Your mama called you, didn't she?"

I don't say anything.

He tries to take a deep breath. It hurts.

"Well, that's all it's gonna be is a little visit," he tells me. He's trying to get himself situated. He doesn't like me seeing him flat on his back. "I don't want you missing any school because of me.

I'm gonna be fine. You hear me? You get in that truck and drive back to Beaumont. I'm not gonna be the cause of you flunking out this time. You hear?"

Same old man. "Yes sir."

"Shawn's at the lot. Your mama's answering the phone. Everything's taken care of."

"How you feeling?" I ask him.

"I'm fine," he says. "I don't know why in the hell they're keeping me here. I could be *in bed* at home."

"You'll be home soon," I tell him.

"And you'll be back at school tonight!" he says. "I ain't shittin' you. I mean it."

"I didn't drive all this way for you to run me out of town as soon as I get here."

"I know," he says. He has his boots right by the bed so that he can find them if he wants to get up and break out of the hospital. "I know. It means a lot to me you came. We'll talk, and then you'll go. Straight to Beaumont. Don't go by the lot. Don't talk to your mama. She'll start whining, and you'll never make it back to school."

We talk for a while about the car business, the economy, school, quail leases, and then he says, "Enough. I'm sleepy. Thanks for coming. Now haul ass."

I wave at him through the small window in the door.

He lifts the fingers of his left hand. There's a tube attached to it.

I'M ABOUT halfway across the long bridge over the Old and the Lost Rivers, and I'm thinking how nice it would be to see Mama and the kid. It would give me a chance to check up on the business.

The old man's lot is on the opposite end of town from the bay.

It's a filling station that he's converted into a used car lot. He cleaned out the grease rack, and Wylie washes cars in there now.

When I pull into the back lot with my U-Haul, I see all the cars on the front line parked crooked. Most of them need washing. I don't see my Oldsmobile anywhere.

Wylie's in the grease rack, chamoising off a station wagon. Wylie's about six-six or six-seven, black, with a shaved head. He dresses like he buys his clothes at the army-navy surplus. When he sees me, he salutes and holds it. "Pleased to see you, sir!" he says with a big grin on his face.

"What's going on?" I say, stopping to inspect him. He's holding the chamois in his free hand. It's dragging the ground.

He's about to crack up. "You done missed all the action, *sir*," he says.

"Cut the bullshit, Wylie," I tell him. "Where's my old car? Y'all sell it?"

"Naw," he says. He's at ease now. "That's what I mean. You missed it."

"Missed what?"

"They stole it."

"Who?"

"Don't know," he says. He's trying to pop me with the chamois.

I grab it away from him. "Talk to me! When'd all this happen?"

"Don't know," he says. He's trying to get the chamois. I'm holding it behind me. "Two guys come in yesterday morning, and the kid let 'em test drive it, and they never come back."

"He inside?"

"Naw, he's gone after 'em."

"*What?*"

"Yeah. Somebody called and said they saw the car somewhere."

I run around front to the office. The old lady's in there signing some checks. "Baby!" she says. She stands up. "When'd you get home?"

"Where's Shawn?"

She looks confused. "Somebody called," she says. "About your car. It was stolen yesterday."

"I know. What'd they say?"

"Who?"

"The guys that called!"

"It was some friend of your daddy's. He said he saw a car that looked a lot like yours pull into The Westerner."

"Call the police," I tell her, running out the door. "Wylie!"

"Yo!" he says.

"Shawn take anybody with him? Junior? Shawn take Junior?"

"Your daddy run Junior off last month."

"He went alone?"

Wylie comes over and whispers in my face. He usually keeps a bottle under the seat of the car he's washing. "He took your daddy's pistol. Don't tell him I told you."

I toss the chamois at him and start running for the truck. "Keep an eye on Mama!" I shout back at him.

"Will do," he says.

I'm backing out of the driveway. "And straighten up the front line!"

He stands at attention. "Yes sir!" he shouts back, laughing. And then he says, "You been by to see your daddy?"

THE WESTERNER is the old drive-in theater north of town not too far from Black Duck Bay. It has been closed for about ten years.

They shut it down right after I got out of high school, and then some business reopened it for a while to show X-rated movies.

From the park across the bay, you could see the back of the screen, the giant yellow neon Stetson, and above in red cursive, "The Westerner." On a still night you could see these things reflected in the bay. You could drive down past the picnic area after a movie and park down close to the water and in between whatever, you might notice them turning off the sign.

Last summer, the hurricane blew the screen over. It's lying now across the playground at the front of the parking area. The Stetson shattered.

Without thinking, I stop for a moment at the ticket office. I can remember my first date here. I can't remember the girl I was with, but I can remember the movies. It was all-night Westerns. *Shane* and *High Noon*. *Big Jake* and *Red River*. *The Magnificent Seven*. It was a night filled with gunfire. I'm thinking of the scene when John Wayne tells Richard Boone, "Now you understand. Anything goes wrong, anything at all, your fault, my fault, nobody's fault, it don't matter, I'm gonna blow your head off. It's as simple as that." I'm thinking of when James Coburn tells the rest of the Seven, "Nobody throws me my guns and tells me to run. Nobody." What made that movie was the sound of the gunshots echoing off the mountains.

I'm hearing them again. Shawn! I drive through the entrance to see where they're coming from. There's a small house way in the back corner where the caretaker lived at one time. There's the old man's truck. There's my car parked in front of the house. I can see someone squatting behind the car. It's Shawn.

I take off across the furrows of parking rows, dodging the speaker poles. With every bump, I'm leaving the seat, bouncing my head off the roof of the cab. About halfway back, I lose the U-Haul, just past the snack bar.

Someone's sticking a gun barrel out of one of the windows of the house. Someone's shooting at Shawn. Shawn's popping up and shooting back, just like in the movies.

I start honking my horn. When I skid to a stop beside the old man's truck, the guy in the house points his shotgun at me.

"Look out!" Shawn shouts, and as I dive down into the floorboard, the windshield explodes. I just lie there for a while, saying *"Goddamn"* over and over to myself.

I open the passenger door and crawl out and peek around the back end of the truck. Shawn is sitting on the protected side of the car with his back up against the right front wheel. He sticks the old man's pistol up over the hood of the car and fires at the house without aiming. He's laughing. "Hey big brother!" he says. "When'd you get home?"

There's a shallow, muddy ditch between us, separating the yard of the house from the parking area.

"What the fuck are you doing!" I shout at him.

A pistol sticks out the front door and fires at the car, blowing out the front tire opposite Shawn. The car is leaning to that side now.

There are two men in the house.

Shawn holds the pistol up again and fires off four more rounds. "What do you think I'm doing?" he says. "I'm getting you your old car back. These niggers stole it."

Keeping low, I run over behind the old man's truck. "I'm not worried about that car. I'm worried about you getting your head blown off. Now get out of there!"

Shawn's reloading. "No way, José. No can do. No es posible," he says. "The old man'd want your car back. He's in the hospital, you know."

Some seagulls are flying over from the bay, crying, high above us.

"Hey," he says, "you better bring me some more shells. I'm getting low." He points. "They're in the truck."

"I'm not getting involved in this," I tell him. "Your ass is in a whole lot of trouble! The old lady called the police. They're on their way."

"Good," he says. "I've got everything under control here."

Just then, the shotgun and the pistol open up on the car. One blast blowing out both windows on the driver's side. They have figured out that I don't have a gun.

They are shooting under the car, trying to get him with a ricochet like in the movies. Shawn's hiding from the bullets. He has both arms wrapped around his head.

They are really opening up on him now, firing one right after the other. A blast, shattering the outside rearview mirror, throws shards of glass at my feet.

Where are the goddamn police! I crawl down to the driver's door of the old man's truck. There are three boxes of shells left. In the rifle rack, there is the old man's over-and-under twenty-gauge. I grab it.

Everything gets quiet again. They must be reloading. I check the shotgun. It only has one shell in the upper chamber.

Shawn's squatting now facing the house, peeking over the hood.

"Stay down, hot shot!" I tell him. "I'm coming over."

One of the black men is shifting his position to the other side of the window. Shawn jumps up and fires at the man, hitting him in the chest with the second shot. The black man falls back into the house.

"Daddy?" someone shouts inside. "Daddy!"

"What are you doing, you stupid little bastard!" I shout at him. "That's murder right there! That's what it is!"

Shawn has a grin on his face. "One down, one to go," he says. "Come on with those shells, man."

It's time for me to make my move over to Shawn. Run, stay low, jump the ditch, and dive behind the car. Nothing to it. I'm looking at the car now, thinking, it won't be worth much when we get it out of here. Shot to pieces, no windows left on either side. Both front and back doors...

"Hey!" I shout over. "Hey Shawn! That ain't the car, man!"

"What?" he says. Everything's still quiet in the house. Shawn's taking pot shots at all the front windows, blowing out the ones that haven't already been broken. When the curtains are hit, they jerk back like someone's in there pulling on them.

"I said, that ain't even the car! My car's a two-door. Count how many that one has!"

Shawn looks back at me with a startled expression on his face. "No shit?" he says. He gets to his feet and stands up to check out the doors.

"Get down!" I shout as a blast comes from one of the windows, catching Shawn in the chest, picking him up and dropping him down on his back in the middle of the ditch.

"Wait!" I drop the boxes of shells and grab the twenty-gauge and run for him. About halfway there, the other black man comes running out of the house, firing his pistol at me, blowing out one of the old man's headlights.

Without thinking, I pull the trigger, and the blast takes him in the right shoulder and spins him around. As he falls, he fires another round into the dirt.

"Shawn?" I say, kneeling in the ditch beside him. The brown water is only about three inches deep. He is staring straight up into the sky.

The gulls are still crying.

Away across Black Duck Bay, I can hear the sirens coming. The black man is trying to crawl back to the front door of the house.

I'm holding the old man's twenty-gauge in one hand and wiping the mud off of Shawn's face with the other.

WHEN THE GODS WANT
TO PUNISH YOU

Watch out, you might get what you're after.
Talking Heads
Stop Making Sense

HEN THE gods want to punish you," I tell him,
"they answer your prayers."

"No shit," Donnie says. He's sitting at the bar between Debbie and Madison.

I'm standing in the kitchen, salting his glass.

"More lime this time," Madison says. She hands me her glass.

Donnie points to his. "More tequila," he says.

Debbie isn't drinking. She's pregnant.

Cazadores

Corazón

Don Julio

Herradura

Patrón

Porfidio

I hand him his drink.

"You know," he says, "I always wanted to be a fireman."

"Dear god," Madison says. She reaches for her glass. "Hurry."

Debbie hides her face in her hands.

"No," Donnie says, "I'm serious."

"We know," Debbie says through her fingers.

"Ever since I was a little kid."

Madison mouths the words, "Fire engine."

"I even had this little fire engine," he says. "Most little kids had little race cars, but I had a fire engine!"

"Was it red?" Madison says.

"It *was* red!" Donnie says. He looks at her. He's holding his head in his left hand, and then he's holding his head in his right hand. "It wasn't a toy," he says. "I mean, you could climb into it. It had pedals and everything. You know what I'm talking about?"

"We know," Debbie says. She lowers her hands and smiles at him.

"Tell us about the bell," Madison says.

"You saw it!" Donnie says.

"No," Madison says.

"Tell me the truth," Donnie says. "Did you ever see it?"

"No," Madison says, "I'm sorry."

"It had this little bell," he says. "Hell, I used to pedal that fire engine up and down our street, ringing that goddamn bell like crazy. Up and down the street. Back and forth." Donnie's pulling this invisible cord on this invisible bell. *"Ding ding ding ding ding ding ding,"* he goes. "All goddamn day."

"You're lucky somebody didn't shoot you," I tell him.

"Terry," Madison says.

"Can't you just picture it!" I say. "Some little maniacal bastard riding up and down the street, dawn to dusk, ringing this goddamned fire engine bell!"

"It wasn't *that* loud," Donnie says.

"Children!" I say.

"Terry," Madison says.

"Aren't children great!"

"Terrence."

[117]

"Don't get me started on children!" I say. "I mean, what cretins would ever *want* to have children unless they had guns to their...."

"I think Debbie needs another drink," Madison says.

I throw Madison a stupid look and say, "Debbie's not drinking! She's...!"

"LET'S JUST say there's a field," Donnie says. "It's nighttime."

"I need another Coke," Debbie says. "Please."

"The field is dark because the sun has gone down," he says. "It's about knee-deep in these black weeds."

"Black weeds?" Madison says.

"I told you!" he says. "It's dark!"

"Nighttime," she says.

"Anyway," he says, "in the middle of this black field, there's a small red fire."

"Call the fire department!" Madison says. She picks up the telephone receiver.

"That's right!" Donnie says. "I rush to the field with my bucket of water and put the fire out."

Debbie applauds.

"What could be more perfect than that?" Donnie says.

Madison finishes her drink. "It's not always that easy, is it?"

"That's not the point," he says. "The point is.... Anyway, that's what I used to dream about when I was a kid."

"When I was a kid," I tell him, "I used to dream about setting those fires."

"LET'S JUST say your house is on fire," Donnie says.

"Call the fire department!" Madison says. She picks up the receiver.

"*Our* house?" I ask him.

"*Somebody's* house is on fire," he says.

"What's their name?" Madison says. "Maybe we should call them."

"Who?" he says.

"*The people in the burning house,*" she says.

Donnie throws his hands in the air. "Help, help," he says, "our house is on fire!"

Debbie's laughing.

"Call the fire department!" Madison says. She hands Donnie the receiver and starts dialing 911.

"Don't do that!" he says. He reaches and hangs up the phone. "Let's just say the fireman gets the call, slides down his pole, jumps in his truck, and he's there. The house is consumed in flames."

"*With* flames," Madison says.

"He jumps out of his truck, hooks his hose to the hydrant, and starts spraying water on the house."

"A simian could do it," I tell him.

"Unless somebody's in there," Madison says. "Unless somebody's in the house."

"That's my point!" Donnie says. "Let's just say there's a baby in the house."

"Christ, Donnie!" Debbie says.

"Don't worry, Sweetie," he says. He reaches and kisses her cheek. "I'm gonna save it!"

I down my drink. "Chihuahuas," I tell him.

"Chihuahuas?" he says.

"Why don't we sprinkle in some Chihuahuas?" I say. I look at Madison. "I've never liked Chihuahuas."

"They wrap this wet blanket around me, and I run into this burning house."

"The way their skin starts to twitch," I say, "just before they bite you. Don't get me started on Chihuahuas!"

Donnie looks at me. *I'm saving this baby if you don't mind.*

"Please," I say, "the house is collapsing all around you."

"That's my point!" he says. He hands me his glass. "We're all gonna die, and what better way to go than trying to save a baby?"

"Come here, Sweetheart," Debbie says. She puts her arms around him and kisses him. "I love you."

"Hurry," I tell him, "before those fucking Chihuahuas follow you out!"

"Anyway," Donnie says, "you're outside, throwing water on the house. It's consumed with flames."

"*By* flames," Madison says.

"The fire has spread across the roof. You got there as fast as you could, but it's fully involved. It's too late. The house is gonna burn right down to the foundation, and there's not a goddamn thing you can do about it. I mean, every rafter, every joist, two-by-four, two-by-twelve—it doesn't matter—every goddamn piece of furniture burned until there's nothing left but two white commodes sticking up out of the ashes."

I hand him his drink.

"Except that you're doing *something,*" he says. "You're *trying* to save it. You're out there all night, throwing water on it, long past the point when you know that it's lost. You're not like the neighbors, standing in their robes, standing in their yards, staring at the flames, their hands in their pockets."

"Aren't neighbors great!" I tell him. "Don't get me started on neighbors!"

"And when it's all over," he says, "no fire, no flames, when all that's left of their house is just hissing—let's just say it's dawn—the people stumble over in their pajamas, crying, hugging each other, and they thank you. They thank you for doing *something*. They thank you for at least *trying*."

"A DEAD soldier!" I tell them. I hold up the bottle of liqueur.

"Road trip!" Donnie says. He pours himself off of his stool.

"It's way too late for that now," Debbie says. She keeps him from falling.

"Not to worry," I say. "We'll have to improvise. Besides, too much liqueur ruins the margarita."

"No chance of that now," Madison says.

I collect the glasses. "Tell them," I say.

Debbie looks at Donnie. "Do I know about this?" she says.

"Tell them about the refinery," I say. "Tell them about the end of the world."

"How do *you* know about the refinery?" Debbie says.

"He worked out there," Donnie says.

"I put my way through school out there."

"In the summers," Madison says.

"I spent one summer out there painting curbs," I tell them. "All day long. From 7:00 in the morning until 5:00 in the afternoon. From May until September. Crawling backwards on my hands and knees through the heat of the summer for miles and miles and miles."

Donnie's laughing. "College boy," he says.

"I mean, once you've painted about five miles of curb," I say, "you know every fucking thing you need to know."

I hand him his drink. "How is it?" I ask him. "The new recipe?"

He sips it and frowns. "Nasty," he says.

"Your supervisor, your foreman, coming out every now and then to check on you. He'd sit there in his golf cart and watch you.

He'd bring a calendar with him, and he'd say, 'Sure is hot!' He'd say, 'Let's see: three and a half more months, fifteen more weeks, seventy-five more days!' And then he'd just drive off. He'd just drive off and shout over his shoulder, 'Don't get too hot, now!' "

"College boys!" Donnie says. "Most of the guys out there didn't finish high school. And we get these college boys for two or three months out of the year, and we're thinking one year from now, maybe two, these boys'll be wearing ties. They'll have good jobs—air-conditioned. They'll be bankers and doctors and lawyers."

"Tell them about the buildings," I say. "The way they're named."

Donnie smiles. "They're not called what you'd think," he says, " 'The Paint Shop' and 'The Welding Shop' and 'The Carpenter Shop.' They're called, 'A Building' and 'B Building' and 'C Building.' "

"Tell them why," I say.

"Christ," Madison says, "you'd better fix me another drink! This is beginning to sound like a GRE question!"

"If anything ever happens," Donnie says, "if there's a fire or a big explosion, you're supposed to report to *your* building. Aikman would go to 'A Building.' Brady would go to 'B Building.' Culpepper would go to 'C Building.' "

"I knew it," Madison says. *"Hurry."*

"For what purpose?" Debbie says.

"For a body count," I say. I hand Madison her drink.

"So they'll know who's dead," Donnie says. "So they'll know who's still out there."

"But it's a joke, right?" I ask him. "They're not serious?"

"They're serious," Donnie says.

"Tell me it's a joke," I say. "You're working out there, you're hard at work, you're only about half paying attention to what you're doing, and you hear this roar, this explosion, and the concussion knocks you to the ground, and you look up, and everybody's running for the fence."

"You'd feel the concussion first," he says.

"I mean, you've got welders and pipe fitters, carpenters and engineers, all running for the fence. Because when that refinery goes, it's going to take the Gulf Coast with it."

Donnie's laughing. "So everybody's hauling ass for the fence," he says. "And they don't even climb it...."

"You don't have time to climb it!"

"You got about five thousand men jumping on a fence at once," he says, "and their weight just carries it over."

"And then it's the mad dash for the water!"

"And then it's the Mile Mad Dash for the Bay," he says, "with the whole fucking world blowing up behind you!"

" 'A Building,' my ass!"

"You don't slow down," he says. "You don't even stop when you hit the water. You just keep running until you can't anymore, until it gets too deep to run."

"All you can see," he says, "all around you, are these hard hats just above the surface. White for painters. Green for welders. Yellow, electricians. Red, firefighters. All of you up to your safety glasses in the salt water."

"As LONG as I can remember," Donnie says, "my old man was a firefighter. He worked at just about every refinery up and down the Channel."

I hold up the bottle of Herradura. "We have enough for one more," I tell them.

"Is that it?" Madison says.

"Then we have to get going," Debbie says. She puts her arm around Donnie.

"I can remember my old man bringing these things home," he says. "A helmet, a charred fire ax, a Dalmatian puppy."

"I've been meaning to talk to you about those dogs," I tell him. "You really ought to bathe them every now and then. You know, spray them down. Scrub some of that goddamned soot off of them."

"I always wanted to be a fireman," Donnie says, "and because he wound up at the refinery, I started out there. I painted hydrants for the first two years. Every goddamn day!"

"*El fin!*" I tell them and hand them their drinks.

"*El fin!*" Madison says, and we toast the end.

"We need to go soon," Debbie says.

"Do you know how many hydrants we got out there?" he says. "It's the biggest fucking refinery in this hemisphere!"

"Good for you," Madison says. She touches her glass to his. "You're starting at the top."

"That's what I tell him," Debbie says.

"That's my point!" Donnie says. "It *is* the biggest. It *is* the best. It *is* the most efficient."

"Your father would be proud of you," Debbie says.

"That's just it!" Donnie says. "It's too clean. It's too efficient. It's too safe."

"Donnie," Debbie says.

"Nothing ever happens," he says. "No alarms. No explosions. No fires."

"When the gods want to punish you," I tell him.

"No shit," he says. "So we just sit around all day and play with our hoses."

"So *that's* what's going on in those stations!" I say.

Donnie beckons me to come closer. He drapes an arm around Debbie and Madison. We huddle together. He whispers, "I have this dream about setting a fire."

"*Donnie,*" Debbie says. She tries to pull away.

He pulls her back. "So we'd have something to do," he says.

"A little one?" Madison says.

Donnie grins. "No," he whispers. "A big one! A real big one!"

"*Donnie!*" Debbie says.

"Out at the refinery," he says. "The biggest fucking fire in the history of the world!"

I look at Madison. Madison looks at me.

"We sit around at lunch and talk about it," he says.

"We need to go," Debbie says.

"But then," Madison says. She pulls away from the huddle. "But then, you'd be good enough to put it out. You'd be good enough to save us."

"Of course!" Donnie says. "That's what firefighters do! They fight fires!"

"The entire refinery?" Madison says.

Donnie downs his drink. "Why not?" he says. "We'd make sure of it. We know all the hot spots."

"You'd be killed," Madison says.

"Good," he says. "Good."

Debbie grabs his arm and says, "Time to go."

"Better to die sprinting into fire than to die drooling in bed!"

"Go to the study," I tell Madison, "before it's too late!"

She spills herself off of her stool.

"Collect all of my students' assignments!"

"Why?" she says.

"Collect all of your students' assignments!"

She's smiling.

"Donnie!" I say.

"Yes, sir!" he says. He salutes.

"Find the water hose!"

"Will do!" he says. He walks out back.

"Debbie!" I say.

She's frowning.

"Listen, Debbie," I say, "you are crucial to the implementation. Here are the matches. Go into the garage and find the barbecue pit. Bring us the lighter fluid, please."

She's just looking at me.

"Hurry," I tell her, "there's not a second to lose!"

Donnie's left the back door open. I walk out into the yard. "How are we doing out here!" I say.

"I found the hose!" he says from somewhere in the darkness.

"Good!" I tell him. "Take it around front!"

There's a wheelbarrow leaning up against the back fence. I grab it and start pushing it toward the house.

"Everything?" Madison shouts from the study.

"Everything!" I tell her. I'm having trouble getting the wheelbarrow through the back door. "Every goddamned thing!" I tell her. "Notebooks, note cards, rough drafts, revisions, diaries, journals, outlines, footnotes, endnotes, bibliographies, research papers, essays, personal, expository, comparison/contrast, how-to...." I'm ramming the wheelbarrow into the door frame. "How-to-get-a-wheelbarrow-inside-your-wheel-house!" I'm backing up and getting a good run at it.

Debbie's standing in the middle of the den. She's holding the lighter fluid in one hand, the matches in the other. She's looking at me like she's never seen anything like this in her whole fucking life. "Madison," she says, "you'd better come in here!"

"Students!" I say.

Madison runs into the den. "Terry!" she shouts.

"Aren't students great!" I say.

"Terrence," she says. She's blocking the doorway with her body. "We don't need the wheelbarrow in the house."

"Those goddamned students!" I say.

"I know," she says.

I'm standing in the middle of the yard, holding the wheelbarrow, preparing for another run at it as soon as she steps out of the way. "If it weren't for the students," I tell her, "teaching would be great!"

"I know," she says. "Let me have the wheelbarrow."

"Don't get me started on students!"

I'M STRETCHED out on the sofa, listening to the stereo. I'm watching the angels dance, and I don't know why but I'm thinking about Electric Football.

Madison's in the kitchen preparing these muffins. She's in the kitchen preparing these Pillsbury blueberry muffins. She has this theory.

The muffins aren't for breakfast. It's 3:47.

She has this theory that if she can attach something *cute* like muffins to something *ugly* like tequila she won't get sick.

"Good luck!" I shout over the stereo.

She has this theory that if she *completely* fills her stomach with these warm, sweet, moist Pillsbury blueberry muffins that they will in effect soak up all of the tequila, and she won't vomit.

"Good luck!" I shout. I'm in the den, watching the angels, listening to the Talking Heads.

The amplifier's set at 8.7. It's never been above 9. I remember reading a warning somewhere, something about the speakers, something about losing structural integrity somewhere around 10.

Every now and then, in between songs, I'll shout out, "MUFFINS," and Madison will walk into the den and kiss me on the forehead and say, "Why don't you turn that thing down!"

We had this game when we were kids. It was called Electric Football. There was this metallic board about the size of a desk top. It was green. It was the football field. It had yard markers and everything.

There were two teams of football players. Every position. Plastic. Miniature, of course. Maybe each player was two inches tall. It didn't matter which position you played—you were two inches tall!

Each player stood on his own little stand, a pedestal, kind of like on a plastic army man except that each of these stands stood on its own little feet—little feelers—like the legs of a centipede.

The two kids flipped a coin to decide which team would start on offense. They arranged their players on the line of scrimmage. Centers, guards, tackles.

The football was a wedge of felt you stuck under the arm of your quarterback. He was the player with his other arm sticking straight out in front of him. His legs frozen in the midst of a sprint.

This game, this football game, was unlike any other because it was indeed *electric*. The board, the big green playing field, had a cord. One of you just plugged it into the wall.

There was a switch on the cord, and the kid on offense flipped that switch when he was ready. My little brother had these absurd signals. "20 Blue!" he would shout. "20 Blue! 14 92! 17 76! 18 12!

20 Blue! 18 36! 18 61! 18 98! 20 Blue! 19 14! 19 39! 19 41!" before he would ever say, "Hike!" and flip the switch. "20 Blue!" he would shout. "20 Blue!" until you finally had to reach over and slap the shit out of him.

"Hike!" he would finally say, and he would flip the switch, and the play would start. The entire board, the entire playing surface, the entire football field would start to vibrate and hum, and all of the players, offensive and defensive, would spring into motion.

The play was not over, the quarterback not down, until he was *touched* by a player on the opposing team. The ball was not dead until one of the defensive players *bumped* into your quarterback.

You could design your plays. You could set up elaborate end runs with pulling guards, intricate sweeping reverses, wicked draws. But what made Electric Football fascinating was that you could not predict what your players would do—how they would move, where they would go.

You spent minutes meticulously lining them up, pointing them in the right direction, placing them in their proper positions, and then you flipped the switch, the whistle blew, and it became the Bedlam Bowl.

Sometimes, well-intentioned, seemingly competent centers quickly pivoted and began blocking the quarterback.

Sometimes, guards and tackles hooked elbows and began dancing over a hash mark.

Sometimes, sure-handed, fleet-footed wide receivers sprinted directly off the field and spent the duration of the play butting their heads against the bleachers.

Sometimes, cunning, calculating, carnivorous linebackers pirouetted at midfield.

Sometimes, my league leader in yardage, my Heisman trophy

winner, my number one draft pick, my star running back spent five, ten, fifteen minutes running around in circles, around and around, looking for the ball, looking for the play.

And it never failed—my quarterback, my Bradshaw, Staubach, my Montana, received the snap, faded back and back, faster and faster, until he was running for the wrong end zone where he bounced off of the goal post and started gyrating, slowly at first and then more rapidly, faster and faster, until he dropped the ball.

Down in one end zone, next to the scoreboard, there was a dial that regulated the vibration of the board.

After the two of you had been sitting there watching the same play for thirty minutes, forty-five minutes, and the quarterback still wasn't tackled—the quarterback wasn't even *close* to being tackled (I mean, there wasn't a defensive player within the same zip code, the same county, the same fucking state)—one of you simply turned the dial to increase the intensity of the game. One of you simply intensified the search for the ball.

The owner's manual recommended a dial setting of 3 for optimal game conditions. But you could turn the dial to 6 and increase the vibration of the board. You could turn the dial to 6 and increase the desire of each player.

At the setting of 6, both offensive and defensive players sprint frantically about the field, running in and out of bounds. At the setting of 6, the players, in a panic, spin uncontrollably, their hands in the air. They have forgotten the rules. They can remember the search, but they cannot remember the object of the search.

At the setting of 9, the entire world is shaking. Veteran tight ends fall to their faces. Acrobatic cornerbacks complete full gainers. Safeties fly through the uprights into the stands. Nose tackles lie on their backs in convulsions. The players have long since forgotten the search.

I'M STRETCHED out on the sofa, listening to the stereo, watching the angels dance.

Madison collects angels. She collects crystal angels, pewter angels, angels made of porcelain, angels made of stone. She collects kissing angels, some with halos, most with wings.

They are dancing around on the top shelf between the large speakers. They are fluttering about, brushing their wings against one another. Their halos cocked at precarious angles. The kissing angels are promiscuous. They are switching partners. They peck, and then they flit and flirt, and then they pucker for someone new.

"Angels!" I shout toward the kitchen.

"What!" she says.

"Aren't angels great!" I shout.

"I can't hear you!" she says.

"Don't get me started on angels!"

"Why don't you turn that damned thing down!" she says.

I reach and turn the dial to 9.

The angels, wing tip to wing tip, have huddled together now. They are all facing the same direction. The whole herd of them shuffles slowly toward the edge of the shelf.

DID I hear it or feel it? Without knowing how, I'm off the sofa on my hands and knees on the floor. The stove! "Madison!" I shout over the music. I get to my feet, turn off the stereo, and she's standing right in front of me. "Are you okay?" I ask her, and without thinking, we're holding each other's hands.

"What was that?" she says.

I'm thinking that it was a nightjar, a sea gull, a screech owl flying through the night. The light's on in the den. I'm thinking that an owl flew into the bay window.

"It's all right," I tell her. "Let me go check." I open the back door.

"Be careful," she says.

I'm thinking Barn, Barred, Great Horned Owl. I'm thinking I can pick it up, pet it, hold it for a minute, make sure its head's looking in the right direction, climb up on the roof, and then toss it back into the night.

"The window shook!" she says.

"Why don't you go get the flashlight," I tell her.

I step out into the dark and notice, one by one, lights coming on in the neighborhood.

I'm looking around on the ground, trying to figure out where I'd be if I were a dazed owl, trying to figure out how far most owls bounce.

This time, I both hear it *and* feel it. "Goddamn!" I say. I find myself sitting on the ground.

"Terry!" Madison shouts. She runs out of the back door. "Terry!" She's looking for me with the flashlight.

"Over here!" I say.

"Are you all right?" she says. She shines the flashlight in my face.

"Help me up," I say.

"What was that?" she says.

"An explosion," I say. "Somewhere out there."

I look at Madison. Madison looks at me. We start smiling.

"Call him," I tell her.

"I will not!" she says. "They're in bed by now!"

"Call him," I tell her. "I'll bet he's getting ready. I'll bet he's about to leave."

"Is it the refinery?" she says.

"I don't know," I say. "I'm not sure." She hands me the flashlight. "Call him."

Madison's grinning. *"This is your idea,"* she says and walks back inside.

I climb up on the air conditioner, onto the fence, into the mimosa. I drop down onto the roof. I crawl up to the peak and stand. "Where are you?" I say.

I shine the flashlight toward South America, the Gulf of Mexico, Galveston Island, the bay. "That's south," I say. I move the beam slowly up the Ship Channel. Du Pont. Phillips. Shell. Ethyl. Arco. Exxon. No fire.

I'm thinking of him putting his boots on the wrong feet. I'm thinking of him kissing Debbie goodbye and then hobbling hurriedly out of his house. I'm thinking of him falling off of the fire truck, rolling back home all the way down the road.

I'm standing up on top of the roof. I'm shouting, "Donnie!" I'm laughing. I'm shouting at the tops of my lungs, *"Donnie, you'd better wake your ass up!"*

Madison runs out into the dark. "What is it?" she says. "What's the matter?"

I'm laughing so hard I can barely stand up.

"Where are you?" she says.

"Up here!" I tell her.

"Goddamnit, Terry!" she says. "Get down from there! You're going to fall and break your goddamned neck!"

I take a deep breath, fill my lungs with the night air, tilt my head back, and shout at every fire in the sky, "D O N N I E !"

"To the Bat Poles!" I shout, sliding down the mimosa. I run around the corner of the house. "Phasers on stun!"

She catches me. "Shhh!" she says. "You'll wake the neighbors!"

I look around the neighborhood. There's a light on in every house. "Everyone's awake!" I tell her.

She places her hand over my mouth.

"The truck," I whisper.

"Let me get my purse," she says and runs inside.

I climb up on the picnic table and shout in the direction of Donnie's house, "Call the fire department!"

"I'm coming!" she says. "Would you shut up!"

"Yeah, shut the fuck up!" someone says from across the fence.

Madison's standing at the back door, jingling her keys up over her head.

"Shotgun!"

I roll down the window. "D O N N I E !" I shout into the night. Madison grabs me by the belt and pulls me back inside. "Is your door locked?" she says. "Where are we going?"

I turn on the flashlight and point through the windshield. "That way," I tell her.

"Turn that off!" she says. "I can't see a thing!"

I shine the flashlight through my window. "North," I tell her.

"North?" she says. "There's nothing north!"

"There most certainly is!" I tell her. "Mobay. Mobay is north. Chevron. Chevron is north. And that other big one in Mont Belvieu. The one that's on the salt dome. The one that's always blowing up."

"I hope you know what you're talking about," she says.

WE CROSS the creek on Main Street. We head north, away from the bay. We leave the dead town behind us, the boarded windows, the closed shops, the empty stores.

We can see the interstate in the distance, and we can see the bright lights of the shopping mall pulsing like the town's new heart.

"Malls!" I say.

The vast parking lot vacant. There are two vehicles parked side by side, nose to tail. Security guards.

I shine the flashlight on the two of them. "Aren't malls great!" I say.

"Where are we going?" she says.

"They build a shopping mall," I tell her. "They build a mall, and they run all of the mom-and-pop shops out of business. They suck the living blood out of a town."

"Terrence," she says.

"Don't get me started on shopping malls!" I say.

We leave the lights of the interstate behind us, the stations supplied with gasoline by the refineries up and down the Channel. The mall is only a small dome of light in the distance.

Madison drives on through the early morning into the dark green miles of rice country.

"Terry," she says, *"we're out in the middle of nowhere."*

"This is a short cut," I tell her.

"A short cut," she says. She shakes her head.

I point the flashlight to the northeast. "It should be over there somewhere."

"Should be," she says. *"Somewhere."*

"Stop the truck," I tell her. "Let me get out and check."

"Let's go home," she says. *"This isn't even Donnie's fire."*

She stops the truck. I open the door and hop out. "But he'll be called," I tell her. "It's a big one, and he'll be called to help."

The concussion knocks me back against the truck. The next explosion is so much louder because we're so much closer, because there are no houses, because there are no trees.

An enormous fireball lights up the sky.

"Goddamn!" I shout. I'm pointing. *"Did you see that!"* I run around to the back of the truck. *"Hurry,"* I tell her, *"or we'll miss it!"*

"Get in!" she says.

I climb over the tailgate and walk up the bed to the cab. "I'm in!" I tell her. "Let's go!"

"At least, close your door!" she says.

"It'll close!" I tell her. "Just gun it!"

"Hang on!" she shouts. She stomps the gas pedal, the truck jumps forward, the door slams shut, and I fall on my butt in the bed.

I get to my feet and stand behind the cab.

We're flying up Main Street, past acres and acres of rice fields. The dark green on both sides as far as I can see. We cross a service road every mile down the street. The fields exactly one mile square.

The horizon is ablaze. Another fireball shoots into the sky. The refinery is on the highway, still some ten miles away.

I lean around and shout into the driver's window, "Take a right at the next road! I can see it!"

She takes the corner too quickly, slides off of the road, and almost loses me. "W H O O E E !" I shout.

I lean around again and shout against the wind, "One for left! Two for right!" I demonstrate. I strike the top of the cab like I'm playing a kettledrum. "Left!" I shout.

"Got it!" she says.

I'm looking over the cab at the burning horizon. "DON-NIE!" I shout. "Ready or not, here we come!"

WE'RE FLYING down oyster-shell service roads. I look through the back window, and we're going seventy-five miles per hour. Madison's turn indicator is still flashing. I love this woman! Behind us, billowing clouds of white dust fan out over the fields.

Madison's turned on the stereo. "Louder?" she shouts.

"Louder!" I tell her.

Talking Heads shout out of the window.

I'm standing behind her, my arms stretched out over the cab, singing "Psycho Killer" at the tops of my lungs into the early morning. There are so many dead bugs on my glasses I can't see anything clearly. The road is just a blurry white strip beyond the headlights.

"Swamp" is on now.

We're zigging down service roads, zagging toward the horizon. "Left!" I shout, a rice field later, "Right!" North for a mile, and then for a mile, east.

I'm playing the bongos in "Slippery People" on top of the cab until my fingers are stinging.

A pause. The crowd applauds. And then, the drums. And then, "Watch out, you might get what you're after."

"The muffins!" she shouts, and all of a sudden, the truck is sliding sideways down the road, and directly between beats, my drum is gone, and I am tossed, hurled, ejected, launched.

I'm airborne, soaring high over the dark fields, my arms straight out in front of me just like Superman—not this latest color asswipe—just like the original black-and-white Superman, flying with both arms sticking out in front of me—not like Mighty

Mouse who always had one arm cocked back to punch some fucking cat. "Up, up, and away!" I shout. What was the actor's name, the one who played the first Superman, the one who shot himself to death—not quite faster than a speeding bullet? What was the actor's name, the one who played the second Superman, the one who fell and broke his neck attempting one last jump—not quite able to leap tall buildings in a single bound?

Higher and higher into the sky I fly. Far down below, I can see the light brown rice canals, the light green levees.

Muffins?

I look over my shoulder, and the truck is only a pair of taillights disappearing into the dust.

"Muffins!" I shout out in front of me.

Behind me, the horizon is on fire. I can see the flames. I'm shouting, "Aren't muffins great!"

Higher and higher into the sky I fly—until I can see flames on both horizons, until I can see two fires—up and up to that point where I just stop, still, motionless for a moment, where I feel the first slight tug at my little toe, and before I go, I shout, "Don't get me started on muffins!"

THANKSGIVING

Zebras. Tigers. Neon Tetras.
Angels. Devils. Runny Noses.
Snakeheads. Swordtails. Silver Dollars.

THE TANKS gurgling. I like the sound it makes. I like the blue
rocks. I like the white castle where the little fish can go and hide.

I close my curtain. I turn my light off. I lie on my bed and
watch the tank glow all day long. And at night, when everythings
got quiet, when everybodys gone to bed, I lie there and watch the
fish swim and listen to the bubbles till I fall asleep.

The door opens. Shithead, he says. Wake up.

Im awake, I say.

He turns the light on. Get your ass up, he says.

I climb out of bed. Its up, I say.

You sleeping in your clothes, he says.

I like to be ready, I say.

Lets go, he says. Its almost noon. He grabs me by my ear and
leads me outside.

Almost noon, I say.

Its a bright day. The wreckers parked on the road. The doors
open.

Wheres Squirt, I say.

Sleep, he says.

[139]

Wheres Mama, I say.

He shakes me by my ear. Dont you worry bout your Mama, he says. You hear me.

I hear you, I say.

He picks me up so Im up on my toes. Dont you go bothering her, he says. Dont you go winding her up.

I wont, I say.

He lets go. He reaches in his pocket and pulls some keys out. Go get your Gramma, he says.

Yesir, I say.

Take the duck truck, he says. Stay on the shoulder.

Yesir, I say.

Go get your Gramma and bring her back here, he says. Its Thanksgiving.

Thanksgiving, I say.

Go get your Gramma, he says. Take the duck truck. Stay on the shoulder. You think you can handle that.

I can handle that, I say.

Im going to the shop, he says. The turkeys in the stove. Ill be back afterwhile.

Afterwhile, I say.

He climbs in the wrecker. He closes the door and rolls the window down. He looks out at me. Dont hit nobody, he says. Dont let nobody hit you. You understand.

I understand, I say.

He starts the wrecker. I mean it, he says. You get in a wreck, you better be dead before I find you. You hear me.

No wrecks, I say.

If you dont die on the highway, he says, you can change the oil in the duck truck tonight. Can you do that.

I can do that, I say.

He shifts the wrecker into gear. He points his finger at me. Dont get yourself killed, he says and drives away.

I stand out there and look cross the road. Mr Rockwells got some turkey decoys. I can see them lined up on his porch. Squirt waits till the coast is clear. He waits till Mr Rockwell goes to work, and then he crawls underneath our house and shoots at them. He shoots at them till they fall over. Most of them look pretty close to dead. One aint got a head. One aint got no feet. Hes just sitting there on his bottom. Ones rolled off the porch and all the way down the driveway.

DADDYS GOT a garage. He fixes things. Cars. Trucks. He fixes everything thats broke. He use to work at the house, but then Squirt came along, and EVERYTHING WENT TO HELL.

Squirt use to live with me till Mama got scared that Id kill him. Squirtll do anything you say. Jump off the roof. Jump out a tree. Eat everything. Bugs. Bad berries. Bullets. Pennies. Nickels. Dimes. Guppies. Glass. Hell stick marbles up his nose. Mamad hold him. Mamad run round the house and scream, YOURE GONNA KILL HIM. YOURE GONNA KILL HIM.

No I wouldnt. I wouldnt never. Squirts better than having a dog. Squirts like having a monkey.

So Squirt moved into the garage, and Daddy moved into town. Mama fixed it up nice. Painted it all blue. Cleared out a spot. Put a bed in there. Mama told me to tell Squirt not to touch Daddys guns. Not to turn his machines on. Not to play with his tools. So I told him,

Just in case you got any, dont go blowing your brains out.

Dont go cutting your fingers off.

Dont go drilling holes in your head.

Dont go sawing your body into.

I have to watch him every second, or hell do just that. So Squirt got the garage and the dogs and the guns, and I got my old room back.

I have a secret door. No one else knows bout it in the world. Its like a secret passageway. Its like a secret tunnel outside a dungeon. Its a hole underneath my bed. When everything gets bad in the house, when everyone gets mad, I can climb out of my covers, I can crawl underneath my bed and sneak out.

I walked out to the garage and got a hacksaw blade. I got a tape too and measured myself. I measured myself so that I could get out. I measured the dogs so that they could get in. I waited till Mama took her nap, and then I moved my bed and started sawing.

Mama takes a nap every day thats not a school day. Thats when everythings quiet. Thats when everythings calm. Some days shell sleep for hours, and on those days Ill sneak in there and saw. Its like Im a prisoner. Its like Im escaping.

Mamas a good mama as long as shes asleeping. When shes awake, THERES HELL TO PAY. I have to be careful moving the bed. I have to be quiet sawing the boards. If you wake her up, shell start screaming. Shell start throwing things. Shell start chasing you round, and if she catches you

you wouldnt think it to look at her, but she can hit harder than Daddy. Shes a girl, and girls dont aim. Girlsll hit you where ever they can.

MAMA AINT got no teeth. Not one in her whole head. I looked in there while she was snoring. I got my flashlight that I take out to the blinds and shined it all over the place in there. Nope. One time she was cooking at the stove in the kitchen, and I asked her, Mama, why aint you got no teeth, and she whacked me on the head with a wooden spoon and asked me if Id like to have MY teeth knocked out.

Mamas got false teeth. Mamas got false teeth that she can stick in there and look like a normal person. She can just open her mouth and stick them in there. Theyre bright white. Theyre straight. There aint one cavity. There aint one filling. I asked her if they was human teeth, and she whacked me again.

She takes them out when shes asleeping. She can just reach in there and yank them out. Does it hurt, I say. When she takes them out, she looks like Gramma. When she takes them out, she sounds like a retard. I know not to laugh. But not Squirt. When Mamas awake, when shes storming round the house with no teeth in her head, somethings bout to happen. I know not to look at her. I know not to talk to her. But not Squirt. The second he sees her, the second he hears her talk, he falls on the ground and starts rolling all over the place, and then the dogs start barking, and then its time to run.

I TELL Squirt you gotta keep your eyes open. You gotta keep your ears open. When Mamas mean, when shes awake, you better run. You better hide. When shes in the house, you better not be. You can be tending to your own rat killing, but youre bout to get beat.

I tell Squirt you gotta keep your mouth shut. Squirt dont talk. He can talk. He just dont. I tell him not to. Dont talk, I say. Dont say a word. You can talk to the dogs, and you can talk to me. You talk round here, and youre bout to get beat. It always happens. They shout at you. They scream at you. They ask you questions. And no matter what you say, youre bout to get beat. So Squirt dont talk. Daddyll pick him up by the ear. Daddyll shout in there, Is anybody home. Daddyll drop Squirt down on the ground and say, Just what we need. Nother retard.

It makes Mama mad. Shell pick Squirt up and start shaking him. Talk gotdammit, she says. When Mamas not hugging or kissing on Squirt, shes beating on him. I know you can talk, she says. Ive heard you with the dogs. Shell start shaking him hard, and Ill run up and hug her leg and say, STOP MAMA PLEASE. YOURE GONNA BREAK HIM.

This is why I hide Mamas teeth. This is whatll stop her. When shes beating on Squirt, when shes beating on me, I go for them teeth. Top and bottom. I get them teeth and hide them. In the attic. Under the house. In the dog food. In cans of paint. Buried in the ground. Sometimes when things get bloody, Ill forget where I hid them. Sometimes when were playing outside, up in the tree house, down in the ditch, well run cross a pair, and Squirtll scream, and Ill whack him on the head and say, Thats just Mamas teeth.

MAMAS A school teacher. She teaches school. School teachers need teeth. School teachers cant teach school without no teeth. Mama cant teach school. When Mama cant teach school, SHE gets a beating.

I gotta keep my eyes open. I gotta keep my ears open. If I dont, shell catch me. Shell grab me by my throat and say, Where are my gotdam teeth.

And Ill say, Dont know.

And shell slap me down.

And Ill get up.

And shell say, Where are they.

And Ill say, Dont know.

And shell slap me down and go after Squirt.

And Ill get up and say, You beat him, and youll never see them teeth again.

Nobody beats Squirt but me.

I WALK through the garage before I go. Squirts asleeping with the dogs. You boys look after him, I say. I walk through the house. The dining room. The kitchen. There on the bar is the church key and the four cans of oil for tonight. Mamas asleeping on the ground in the bathroom. I open my door to check on my fishes. The rooms dark, but I can see the Chester drawers. I can see the blue tank glow. Jack Dempsey, I say, keep a lookout. And then I go.

I hate starting the duck truck alone. I gotta choke it. I gotta stomp one foot on the clutch pedal. I gotta stomp the other on the starter, and all this time Im rolling backwards down the driveway cross the road. Sometimes Ill roll over into Mr Rockwells yard. Sometimes Ill roll out into the road and almost hit someone. Sometimes someone almost hits me.

I gotta push the seat back. I gotta stand up when Im driving so that I can see over the dashboard. I stay on the shoulder. I stay in first gear. In the duck truck, the gearshifts on the column, and second gear is sitting right up there next to reverse. Daddy says all it takes is one time shifting from first into reverse, and youll never do it again. The scariest part is the signaling. I gotta let go of the wheel and stick my whole arm out the window.

I DRIVE over the Trinity and through the Thicket to Grammas house. I drive through Ames where the Niggras live, where white people aint allowed to stay. I drive through the deep woods till there aint no trees just fields as far as you can see. Sometimes theyre filled with water, and you can see the blue sky. Sometimes theyre so bright green they hurt your eyes. The dirt levees snaking way off to the ends of the world.

I can see the men out there, black and white, working in the water. Everybodys got his own field. I honk my horn and wave at them. Mr Leo and his men. Mr Lloyd and his. Mr Bob and Mr Joe. Mr Bill takes his hat off and waves back. They all know this truck.

I drive through Raywood with its white castle. Its towers reach the sky. One day, I ask Daddy, Wheres the drawbridge.

Shut up, he says.

I mean it, I say. Where is it.

What, he says.

You know, I say. The drawbridge. The front door. Every castle has one.

You retard, he says. That aint a castle. Thats a dryer. Thats where they store the rice. Thats where they store the grain.

In case they get attacked, I say.

Shut up, he says.

When I get to Devers, I turn by the station with the big green Dino on top. One day, I point and tell Daddy, Thats a bronto-saurus.

You retard, he says. Thats a dinosaur.

MAMAS A school teacher. She teaches first grade. It use to be quiet. It use to be calm. Daddyd get up and go to the garage, and Mamad get up and go to school, and itd just be me and Squirt and the dogs playing all day. But then I grew up and had to go to school. The principle said it wouldnt be fair for me to be in Mamas room, so they stuck me in The Special Class.

The Special Class was great. Everything was Special. We had a Special lunchroom. Plastic forks and plastic spoons. We had a Special playground. A merry-go-round. A jungle gym. All rubber. Everything was short. Everything was close to the ground. Thats so we couldnt fall so far. Thats so we couldnt hurt ourselves.

We were always walking round the school. Lets go for a stroll,

Miss Bingham says, and off wed go. All of us tied together with these ropes so that we wouldnt wander off. Wed walk by Mamas room, and Id knock on the window and wave at my friends that were having to sit in there and learn to read. We were always walking all over the place. Every now and then, theyd load us on a bus and drive us into Houston. Every now and then, theyd drive us to the circus. Every now and then, theyd drive us to the zoo.

The greatest thing was this. No matter what, you couldnt get in trouble. You could walk round all day with a trash can on your head. You could stand on the slide and scream. You could eat your crayolas. You could eat your paste. You could run round on your hands and knees barking like a dog. You couldnt get in trouble. Why. We were Special.

This week, we put our hand down on a piece of paper, and then we trace it, and then we color what we trace. We color the thumb red. Thats the head, Miss Bingham says. We can give it a eyeball if we want to. We color the fingers with different crayolas. The fingers are the feathers, Miss Bingham says. We color the rest of the hand black, and what we got is a turkey.

I DRIVE through Devers to Grammas house. She lives in the woods at the end of the road. I drive into her yard and shift into neutral. I honk the horn. The front doors open. GRAMMA, I shout out the window.

I climb out and run up to the porch. Gramma, I say.

I open the screen and walk inside. Gramma.

I walk through the living room. The dining room. The kitchen. The stoves on.

The back doors open, so I walk outside. GRAMMA, I shout into the woods, and then I see it, not my door open, but hers, and Gramma sitting in the truck.

I laugh and run out to her. I climb behind the wheel and say, Hey Gramma.

And she says, Woody.

Thats right, I say. I shift into first and gun it so hard it slams both our doors. I drive through the trees and back onto the road. Grammas staring straight through the windshield. Woody, she says.

Mam, I say.

I stay in first gear. I stay on the shoulder. I drive the twelve miles back home. And as we pass each field, I honk, and Gramma says, Bill, Joe, Bob, Lloyd, Leo, just like she knows them by heart.

I TURN off the highway, down the road, and when I pull up front, I see Mama lying facedown in the yard in her underwear.

Woody, Gramma says.

Mam, I say, but I dont stop. We got plenty of gas, so I keep on driving, on into town and out the other side to the river bottom where we use to go to church.

Theres cars and trucks parked underneath the trees. I stop over by the graveyard and shift into neutral. I run round and open Grammas door, and she says, Sunday.

Nome, I say. Its Thanksgiving.

I walk her round back where the picnic tables go all the way to the river. I can see the red and white tablecloths. I can see the sleepy moss blowing in the breeze. I can see all my friends in their Sunday school clothes. Come and play, Woody, they say.

Not today, I say.

Mr Preacher walks up and says, Why, Sherwood, this is a surprise.

Yesir, I say, I expect.

Mrs Preacher walks up and says, Wheres your mother.

Resting, I say. This is my Gramma.

Mr Preacher says, Its a pleasure, mam.

And I say, Can she have some turkey with you.

Why, of course, Mrs Preacher says. She takes Grammas arm and says, Come with me, mam.

And Mr Preacher says, I hope youll join us, Woody.

And I say, Maybe next year. And I start running for the truck. Take good care of my Gramma, I shout back at him.

We will, he says. She can have as much turkey as she wants.

I climb in the truck and shift into gear. You gotta cut it up for her, I say. She aint got no teeth.

I TURN the engine off. I shift into neutral and coast up the road. Shes still lying there in her underwear. I open the door, but I dont shut it. I tiptoe up behind her in case its a trap.

Mama, I say. I kick her foot. I walk round and round her. I stay way clear of her at first. She could jump me like a gator.

Hey Mama, I say. I poke her head with my boot. You alive.

Hey, I say. I reach in my pockets. I found these teeth in the back of the commode, I say. I put them together, top and bottom, and hold them in my hand. I squat down so that she can see them.

A car comes down the road and stops behind me. Sherwood, it says. Sherwood.

I stand up and turn round. Its Miss Bingham. Shes dressed up. Hi Miss Bingham, I say.

Is that your mother, Miss Bingham says.

I look at Mama. I think so, I say.

Is she all right, Miss Bingham says. Is she ok.

Shes just fine, I say. I bring my finger to my lips. I whisper, Shes just asleeping.

For gods sake, Miss Bingham says, put something on her. And then she drives away.

Shes right, of course, so I walk to the duck truck and climb in the bed. I find the camo tarp and throw it over Mama. I got her head covered with her feet poking out, and then I got her feet covered with her head poking out, and then I got her whole body covered when I see the front door open and the smoke pouring out.

Shit, I say and run inside. I cant see a thing. The houses filled with smoke. I fall over the coffee table. I get up and find the back door. I throw it open, and the dogs run in. Hey, I say. HEY.

Im swatting at the smoke, trying to find the fire. I run into my bedroom to check on my fishes. Everythings fine. The rooms dark. The blue lights on. No smoke in here yet. Water dont burn. I stick a towel under the door, and then I climb under the bed, and then I sneak through the hole, and then I crawl under the house.

I run into the garage. Squirts still asleeping, so I kick him and say, The houses on fire. The dogsre hopping up and down on the bed. Wake him up, I say.

I drag the box fan into the kitchen and turn it on. Im coughing. My eyesre burning. The fans blowing the smoke round. The dogsre jumping up and down. Wheres the fire, I say.

And then it hits me. The stove. I run over and open the door, and the black pours out. The dogsre barking now. Theyre going crazy like they want to climb in there. SHOO, I say. GO WAY.

I find the stove glove. I hold my breath. I close my eyes and reach inside. I feel the turkey, but its stuck to the pan, and the pans stuck to the stove. I yank and yank and rip it loose. The turkey looks like a burnt football. Im holding the leg till the leg falls off, and whats left of the bird falls on the floor, and the dogs jump on it like its a duck. Theyre barking at it. Theyre biting at it.

Theyre snapping and snarling like they cant decide if they love it or hate it. They take turns dragging it outside. THATS GONNA BE HOT, I say. The turkey leg tastes just bout right.

I LIFT the garage doors, and the sun floods the room with light. The breeze from the rivers blows the smoke away. The dogsre out back with the turkey.

Shithead, I say. Wake up.

Squirt dont move.

You alive, I say. I kick him with my boot.

Squirts the best. He can play dead better than anybody. Even I cant tell. Its like he can stop breathing. When things get bad, when things get bloody, Squirt plays dead.

If youre dead, I say, you better tell me. I aint mouthtomouthing you. You can just die before I do that. You can just die and rot in here. You can just die and rot in here, and the dogsll eat you. You dont think Mama and Daddyll care. They wont care. I wont even care. Maybe the dogsll care, but itll be after they done ate you. Crying round, howling round, sad that youre dead, carrying you round in their stomachs to remind them.

Squirt aint breathing. His heart aint beating.

I aint shitting you, I say. Dont make me tickle you.

Squirt opens his eyes. He sits up. Morning, he says.

Its afternoon, I say. Get your ass up.

Hes rubbing his eyes. Wheres the dogs, he says.

Thingsre bout to get bloody, I say. We gotta get out of here.

Squirts out of the bed in one jump. Hes standing there in his pajamas with the trap door in the bottom. Lets go, he says.

Get in the truck, I say. Ill be there directly.

And hes gone.

I grab my flashlight that I take out to the blinds. I walk through the house one last time. Theres still black smoke pouring out the stove. I move the fan and point it inside.

I walk out back and climb under the house. I can hear the dogs before I see them. Theyre over there somewhere, snapping and snarling. One of them drags the turkey over to ask me if I want some.

No thank you, I say. I poke my head up into my bedroom. I peek my head out from under my bed. The towel worked. Theres no smoke. Jack Dempsey, I whisper, youre on your own.

Squirts in the duck truck. Hes got my door open. Lets go, he says. He stomps on the starter, and I stomp on the gas.

Squirt points at the tarp. Theres a foot poking out. Whos that, he says.

Thats just Mama, I say.

What happened, he says.

Thanksgiving, I say.

We drive through town. Get down, I say, and Squirt hides in the floorboard. The squares empty. The courthouses closed. Everybodys home and happy. We drive on out to Rivers Road.

You can get up now, I say, and Squirt climbs up in the seat.

Wheres my gun, Squirt says.

You mean you left it, I say.

We drive down Rivers Road to the Old and the Lost. Theres a place where these rivers come together and turn into the bay. Theres a place where Rivers Road ends, and you can stand there and look out as far as you can see. Every night Old River pours out the Thicket and pours into Lost River right bout here, and every night right bout here these rivers come together and pour one another into the bay.

I stop where the road runs underneath the water. I grab my flashlight. Squirt jumps out, and we meet at the end of the road.

Wheres my boots, Squirt says.

Hop on, I say. I squat down, and he hops on, and we wade out into the Old and the Lost.

What bout the gators, Squirt says.

Im walking slow and keeping my eyes on the water all round us. There aint no gators, I say.

But you said, Squirt says, you said theres always gators.

Not today, I say. Not on a holiday.

Im ankledeep, and then Im kneedeep, and then Im waistdeep when I see it. Squirts blinds way out there in the water. Its so hid sometimes I cant find it in the cattails. I see it now because of the buzzards. Theres four of them sitting on the corners.

Wheres my gun, Squirt says.

They dont fly for the longest time. Ive never been this close before. Theyre way too big to be birds. Theyre baldheaded. Theyre just sitting there watching us. I stop walking. I hold Squirt tight in case theyre thinking bout snatching him up and flying away.

GET ON, Squirt shouts in my ear, and they take off. They fly right over us. We can feel the wind in their wings. THATS RIGHT, Squirt shouts. GET ON AWAY FROM HERE.

Hey gotdamit, I say and swat at his bottom.

What, he says.

We climb into his blind, and we see why. Its filled with flies. Theres two stringers of dead ducks hanging from the posts. A noose round their necks.

Thats why, I say. I drop him down on the bench.

Thats where they went, Squirt says.

I untie the ropes. You cant tell what kind of ducks they were.

You cant even tell that they were ducks. Somethings been eating on them. I hold them up in front of Squirts face.

Squirt holds his nose.

Its a sin, I say, not to clean your kill. I throw them off into the cattails, and something comes up out of the deep water with big teeth and snatches them.

Im sorry, Squirt says. I know better.

The fliesre gone.

Squirts sitting on the bench with his feet in the water. Stand up, I say. Dont do that.

Squirt stands up on the bench. Hes smiling. Is this a game, he says.

Yes, I say. Its a game. Its a mean game.

He stops smiling. Then I dont want to play, he says.

I know, I say. You dont have to.

Woody, he says.

Here, I say. I give him my flashlight.

But thats yours, he says.

Its yours now, I say.

He turns it on and shines it in my face.

Stop it, I say. Listen to me. I gotta get going.

No, he says.

I gotta, I say. Youll be safe out here. Dont leave this blind. Dont burn that till the sun goes down.

No, he says.

When everything gets quiet, I say, when everything gets calm, Ill come for you.

Its gonna get dark, he says.

I look all round me in the cattails. Keep your feet up out of the water, I say, and then I wade on back to shore.

Im waistdeep, and then Im kneedeep, and then Im ankledeep

[154]

when I hear him shouting, DONT GO BACK. DONT GO BACK THERE.

I look back one last time, and all I can see of him is a little head poking up out of the duck blind, and I shout out, YOU BEST WORRY BOUT YOUR OWN SELF.

I climb in the truck and stomp on the starter. I shift into gear and look through the windshield. I cant see Squirt anymore. I cant even see the blind hid out there in the cattails. All I can see is the buzzards flying in circles up above the bay.

WHEN I pull up to the house, Mr Rockwells standing in his yard. Hes collecting his decoys. Hes holding one like hes holding a baby. Hes frowning at me.

I climb out of the truck and say, I didnt do it. Which is the truth.

Everything looks pretty much like I left it. The front doors still open. The houses still smoking. Mamas still asleeping underneath the tarp.

When I walk inside, the dogs attack. They start jumping up and down. They start running round and round. I show them my hands. Turkey, turkey, I say. Gone, gone.

I walk down the hall and open my door. I reach down and pick up the towel. The rooms dark. The blue lights on. All the little fishes are hiding in the castle. Jack Dempseys swimming back and forth keeping guard.

Jack Dempsey, I say. I put my hand on the glass, and he swims over like hes trying to kiss it. Im very proud of you. You did a fine job.

And then I walk into the living room and stand at the bar. Theres the four cans of oil for tonight, theres Daddys church key, theres Mamas bottles, and theres the phone.

WHEN HE answers the phone, I say, Daddy.

And he says, Who is this.

And I say, Its me.

I know who it is, he says. This important.

Sir, I say.

Moron, he says, thisd better be important.

Yesir, I say.

Moron, he says.

Yesir, I say.

Is this important, he says.

You better come home, I say.

I dont think thats what you want, he says. I dont think you want me to come home.

I dont know what to say.

Do you want me to come home, he says.

Not really, I say.

And then he hangs up.

WHEN HE answers the phone, he says, The house on fire.

HOW DOES HE KNOW.

SHERWOOD, he says, the gotdam house on fire.

Sort of, I say.

Sort of, he says.

Sort of, I say.

Where is it, he says.

What, I say.

THE GOTDAM FIRE, he says.

The stove, I say.

Gotdam turkey, he says. Gotdam Thanksgiving.

I know, I say.

Squirt, he says. Get him out.

Hes out, I say. Hes safe.

The dogs, he says.

Out, I say.

Your Mama, he says.

Shes asleeping, I say.

Let her sleep, he says. Woody.

Sir, I say.

Dont catch yourself on fire, he says.

Yesir, I say.

Dont burn yourself to death, he says.

I wont, I say.

And then he hangs up.

IM STANDING outside when Daddy gets home. He drives the wrecker into the yard.

WHOA, I shout. Im standing in front of the tarp. WHOA.

He honks the horn. GET OUT THE WAY, he shouts. He jumps out of the wrecker and tramples over Mama. He walks right on top of her. He storms into the house, and I storm in after him.

The houses still filled with smoke, but he knows where to go. He stops at the stove, reaches in and grabs the pan, and throws it through the kitchen window. The glass breaks, and the dogs bark. They snap and snarl at the pan and then drag it underneath the house.

GOTDAMIT, he shouts. Hes shaking his hand one minute and knocking me down the next. He turns the sink on and sticks his hand in it. You didnt turn it off, he says.

I get up and rub my chin. Wheres the switch, I say.

He points his wet finger at me and says, Dont be a smartass.

I dont even know what that is.

He turns the sink off. Wheres your Mama, he says.

I dont say a thing.

He grabs me by my ear and starts dragging me through the house. Wheres your gotdam mother, he says.

Outside, I say.

He pulls me into their bedroom and shouts, DARSE.

OUTSIDE, I say.

He leads me through the front door and lets me go. Where, he says.

I grab the tarp and throw it back, but theres nobody there. Shit, I say. I drag the tarp all over the yard. THERES NO MAMA.

Idiot, Daddy says. His hands on his hips.

Im looking on both sides of the tarp. She was right here, I say.

He storms back inside. DARSE, he shouts.

Im looking under the house. Im looking up in the trees.

SHERWOOD, he shouts, and I run through the door. The fans blowing the black smoke away. I run through the house till he catches me. Wheres she, he says.

Dont know, I say, and he knocks me down.

And I get up, and he says, Wheres your Gramma.

Dont know, I say, and he knocks me down.

And I get up, and he says, Wheres Squirt.

Dont know, I say, and he knocks me down.

And I get up, and he says, Im gonna ask you one more time.

Its Tooth Fairy time. My left eyes closed. Im looking at him through my right eye when he says, Whered you take them.

And all of a sudden, I dont know why, I CANT REMEMBER, so I close my eye and say, I dont remember. Which is the truth.

I hear glass breaking, and I open my eye, and Daddys on the floor, and Mamas standing over him, holding a bottleneck.

She kicks Daddy in the head and says, Dont go hitting my baby.

But Daddys up like a tiger. He grabs Mama and throws her into the wall. She slides right down. I help her up. Her noses bleeding. Shes crying black tears.

Sherwood, she says. Darling. She looks at me. Go outside and play. She pats me on top of the head, and then she grabs Daddys bowling trophy and knocks him over the coffee table. Shes smiling. Go on, Sweetheart, she says.

I close the front door behind me. This is when Mama starts ascreaming. This is when the decoys start flying out the windows. Some of thems Squirts decoys. Some of thems mine. Glass breaking. Redheads and Buffleheads. Blue-winged Teals and Green-winged Teals. Ruddys and Pintails. Wood ducks and Mallards. Canvasbacks and Mergansers. Every window in the house.

ONCE UPON a time, I played this game. Squirt helped. Not really. I saw this show with this cat and this rat.

Mama makes some pretty things. She paints these pictures. She cuts them out and hangs them in her classroom. She uses tacks and sticks them to her walls. These aint no normal tacks. Thesere GIANT JUMBO thumbtacks. I saw this once on a TV show.

This was way back long time ago when Squirt lived with me. Back when he was still wearing his diapers. I woke him up in the middle of the night. I piggybacked him into the living room and plopped him into Daddys chair.

Wheres the tree, he says.

What, I say.

Wheres the tree, he says.

Shut up, I say.

Every day when the bell rang, Id leave Miss Bingham and The Special Class and walk to Mamas room. Mama was drawing things. Mama was painting things. Mama was happy when she was at school. Every day, Id walk to Mamas room and take a box of tacks.

I piggybacked Squirt into the living room and plopped him into Daddys chair.

Wheres my present, he says.

Shut up, I say.

I dumped all the boxes on the floor. I started outside Mama and Daddys door. I crawled backwards into the living room. Box after box. Tack after tack. I made sure each was standing up straight. I turned the lights off. I turned my flashlight on that I take out to the blinds. One trillion tacks. The hallway sparkled with them shiny points. The floor looked like some kind of torture device.

Squirt says, This gonna be scary.

No, I say. I shine my flashlight on his face. This gonna be funny, I say. This gonna be the funniest thing you ever saw.

What do we do, he says.

What youre gonna do is this, I say. Youre gonna scream, I say. Youre gonna scream Bloody Murder.

When, he says.

When I tell you to, I say. I turn the flashlight off. I hide behind the chair. ok, I whisper.

What, he says.

scream, I whisper.

Now, he says.

now, I whisper.

scream, he goes.

No, I say. I whack him on top of the head with the flashlight. Scream Bloody Murder.

What does that mean, he says.

Scream like someones hacking you up with a ax, I say.

I dont want to play, he says. This gonna be scary.

Im sorry, I say and reach round and pinch the Holy Hell out of him.

This sets him off, and he cranks out a good one. thats it, I whisper and pinch him even harder, and he takes a deep breath and cranks out nother one. thats more like it, I whisper and dig in with my fingernails, and I cant imagine anybody screaming any louder even if they was being hacked up with a ax.

The bedroom door flies open. The knob sticking in the wall. Daddy comes storming into the hallway in his underwear, and I turn the flashlight on and tell Squirt, Watch this.

When Daddys foot finds the first tack, he bout goes through the roof, and then he comes down on the other foot, and back up he goes again just like that cat on that TV show, and hes hopping round like the floors on fire, and I cant take it anymore, so I say, Here, and I give Squirt the flashlight and fall on the floor and start rolling all over the place.

Daddys tap dancing with tacks, and then he falls down hard.

Woody, Squirt says.

Now Daddys got all them tacks on his back.

Woody, Squirt says.

Now Daddys lying on his side, pulling himself towards us. Just wait, he says over and over.

Woody, Squirt says.

Now Daddys bleeding, dragging himself cross the floor. when I get there, he whispers, Im gonna kill you.

And bout this time I stop laughing, and bout this time Squirt turns the flashlight off, and Im sitting there in the dark, thinking bout Daddy, all bloody, crawling cross the floor, reaching out to snatch us, and Im thinking bout poor Squirt who didnt want to do this anyway, whos sitting up in that chair by himself, and all I can think to do to save him is shout, RUN.

IM WANDERING round the yard, picking the ducks up. Im toting them to the truck and sitting them in the bed. One by one. Duck by duck. See, I say, I told you you could fly.

Whats going on over there. Its Mr Rockwell. Hes standing on his porch. Hes sorting his decoys. What is it, he says.

Thanksgiving, I say.

SHERWOOD. Someones shouting. Its Daddy. SHERWOOD.

Coming, I say. I run inside. Im holding a Bufflehead under my arm like a football. Im coming.

The houses dark. Theres no one in there. The back doors open. Theres holes in the windows where the ducks flew through. Theres a chair with all four legs sticking in the wall. The coffee tables broke. The TVs exploded. daddy, I whisper.

Someone grabs me by the neck and throws me up against the wall. Calling your Daddy, she says. Her lips smeared. Her eyes black.

Shes got me by the throat. This is all your fault, she says.

SHERWOOD, Daddy shouts. Hes out back.

She knocks my head back against the wall. She smiles. Ill get you for this, she says.

SHERWOOD.

She lets go and limps down the hallway.

IM COMING, I say and run out the door.

Hes on his hands and knees, looking underneath the house. Where you been, he says.

I found Mama, I say.

He stands up. He slaps his knees with his hands. Shithead, he says.

Yesir, I say.

You did this, he says. He stretches his arms wide. You did all this. You made this mess, and now youre gonna clean it up.

Clean it up, I say.

He steps towards me, and I step back.

DONT YOU DARE RUN, he says. YOU STAND YOUR GOT-DAM GROUND. YOU TAKE WHATS COMING TO YOU.

Yesir, I say.

Listen to me, he says. I gotta get back to the shop. I gotta lock up. But Ill be back. Ill be right back. You hear me.

I hear you, I say.

And you know what youre gonna do, he says.

Nosir, I say. Which is the truth.

He shakes his head. We shoulda just drownt you at birth, he says. He takes a deep breath. Youre gonna fix this, he says. Youre gonna fix all this fore I get back.

Fore you get back, I say.

He points his finger at me. I mean it, he says. Find your Gramma. Find Squirt. Find the turkey. This is Thanksgiving, gotdamit.

Thanksgiving, I say.

He makes a fist, and I close my eye, and I keep it closed till I hear him breaking glass back inside. I stay out there till I hear the wrecker, till I cant hear it screaming down the road.

I PEEP my head through the back door. Everythings dark. I squint my eyes. mama, I whisper.

Everythings quiet. I can hear the dogs snoring underneath the house.

mama, I whisper. I tiptoe inside. mama. I gotta be careful. Theres glass all over the floor. The living room smells like Mama shouting. I can see Daddys broke Mamas bottles. I can see something shiny sitting on the bar. Its Daddys church key, and maybe for a second Im thinking bout tonight, and then Im running down the hall shouting, MAMA.

I stop outside. My doors open. My rooms dark. O Mama, I say. I can hear the pump, but I cant hear the gurgling.

I step inside, and theres the tank on the Chester drawers, and theres the four cans of motor oil.

The tanks filled right up to the brim. The oils a black blanket sitting on top of the water. I cant see the blue rocks on the bottom. I cant see my little fishes anywhere. I look all over the place. I look in the white castle where I would go and hide.

I grab my net and scoop them out. My zebras. My tigers. My neon tetras. I cant tell one from the other. Theyre just laying there on their sides in the tar.

I run into the bathroom and fill the sink. I run back and forth with my net. One by one. Fish by fish. I wash them off, but its too late.

I turn my light on in case I missed one, and there he is on the floor, halfway cross the room, Jack Dempsey. I can see the splash where he landed. I can see the oil he left behind. I can see the trail where he was trying to get underneath my bed, trying to get to my tunnel, trying to get to my secret passageway, and if he got that far, he could escape.

◆◆◆◆◆◆◆◆◆◆◆◆◆◆◆◆◆◆◆◆◆◆◆◆◆◆

OPEN SEASON

EUGENE

WHEN EUGENE answers the telephone, his uncle tells him, "Your truck's ready."

"No kidding?" Eugene says. "So soon?"

Eugene's truck has been dieseling on him. It won't stop running when he turns it off. It's pretty embarrassing for him at school. He gets out of the truck, holding his books, and just stands there, staring at it, waiting for it to die. *And* the driver's door is busted. It won't open from the inside, and every time Eugene closes it, it locks itself. The little locker knob is broken off inside the door, so whenever Eugene wants to get out of the truck, he has to roll the window down and reach out with the key and unlock the door from the outside.

Eugene says, "Y'all had the timing adjusted, the door fixed, and everything?" He left it with them that morning.

"Sure," his uncle says. "Your daddy said for you to get on down here and get it out of our way. When are you coming?"

EUGENE LIVES in a garage apartment close to the junior college, not too far from the car dealership. As he's walking, he's thinking how strange it is that his truck is fixed so soon. Eugene has worked at the dealership off and on as a porter, and he knows that the customers' cars are the first taken to be repaired. And he knows that they had to take the truck to a mechanic for the timing adjustment and then clear across town to the glass company for the door lock problems. All in one day?

So Eugene is ready for something when he walks up on the back lot, and everybody is standing around the front of his truck, under the large oak, his daddy, his uncle, Wylie, and the Mexican. All of them with big grins on their faces. They even have the driver's door open for him. The key in the ignition.

Eugene climbs in the truck, closes the door, and reaches for the key. He's watching them through the windshield, and they're all laughing now, his daddy and his uncle hunched over with their hands on their knees. The Mexican is saying, "Genie boy" over and over again.

Eugene is thinking that something is going to happen. He's thinking, When I turn the key, this truck is going to blow up. This truck is going to blow completely up. Or maybe they've wired a loud siren under the hood that will go off. Or maybe they've loosened all my lug nuts so that my wheels will fall off before I get down the street.

Eugene closes his eyes and starts the truck, and it *still* idles roughly. He tries the door and it won't open, so he rolls the window down to tell his daddy that it still doesn't work, but there are tears in his daddy's eyes. Something is tugging on Eugene's pants leg, so he looks down, and there is an alligator lying in the floorboard on the passenger side. It is not a very large alligator, only about three feet long, but it has Eugene's right pants leg in its mouth, and it's shaking its head from side to side very quickly. Eugene is screaming, throwing himself up against the driver's door. The door handle breaks off in his hand, and the next thing

Eugene knows, he's halfway out the driver's window, hanging upside down, and those that aren't leaning up against the old oak tree are lying on the ground, laughing.

LATER, HANNAH calls him. "What are you up to?" she says.

"Not much," Eugene tells her. He is trying to read and talk to her at the same time. "Just doing a little homework," he says. He is reading an article for an assignment in zoology. His assignment is to write a report on an article that interests him. He has gone through three issues of *Scientific American* before finding an article he can understand. Eugene is reading about imported African bovine dung beetles. "Australians are concerned that their country is being increasingly overrun by cow patties," Eugene writes. "These new alien dung beetles are single-handedly saving Australia."

"Well then, I won't keep you," she says. "I just called to tell you I'm a little excited today."

"Really?" Eugene says. "Why's that?" He is looking at illustrations of the little beetles pushing jawbreaker-sized balls of dung all over Australia. They bury them, somewhere. They are standing on their front legs and pushing the balls with their back legs.

"Why," Hannah says, "it's my birthday." She says, "Today."

Eugene closes the magazine. "Sure it is," he says. He reaches over to his typing stand and jerks the junior college calendar from beneath two books on Texas politics. The nineteenth. "Sure," he says. "I was going to wait and call you a little later. Tonight. After supper. When Daddy gets home."

"Anyway," Hannah says, "that's not why I called. I just talked to your father, and he said that he's picked me up a birthday present, and that it's pretty special, and that I should call you because you've seen it. The only clue he would give me was that I've probably never had anything like it before."

HANNAH IS in the back yard, squatting next to the birdcage. Eugene is on the patio. He closes the sliding glass door. She has not heard him. He has left a duffel bag of dirty clothes in the utility room. A present for her on the bar. He is standing there with his hands in his pockets.

It is a hot late afternoon. Eugene watches his mother wipe perspiration from her brow with the back of her thumb. Far in the back corner of the pasture is a stand of pine trees. There are some crows in the trees, cawing.

The birdcage is tall enough for Hannah to walk into without stooping. It is eight by eight feet, welded out of angle iron. There are broom handles run through the chicken wire at the corners. There is a four-bedroom, two-story birdhouse wired near the top of the cage. It has a verandah. There are close to twenty doves in the birdcage, white, mourning, ring-necked. Some of them on the broom handles, some on the roof of the verandah. They take turns cooing.

Eugene remembers going to sleep to this cooing, something as relaxing as falling rain.

Hannah is wearing one of Bass's white cotton shirts. She has folded back the sleeves to her elbows. The shirttail is out. She is wearing jeans. She is talking to something in the bottom of the cage. "You're going to have to eat something, now. You hear me?" She waddles around the corner. "Hey you," she says and blows through the chicken wire.

Eugene laughs to himself. He walks back to the glass door, opens it quietly, closes it hard. "Happy day after your birthday," he says loud enough for her to hear him. He walks out to her. "Some more babies hatch?"

Hannah stands. "Hi, Sweetheart," she says. "No." She is smiling. "Yes, more babies have hatched. They're in the garage." Some of the old birdseed in the cage has grown into two-foot stalks of maize. "But you've already seen this baby from what I hear." There, lying among the maize, is the small alligator.

"Yes," Eugene says. "We've met."

"Isn't he a cutie?" Hannah says.

Eugene bends over to get a closer look. "Your doves safe with him in there?" he says.

"I think so," Hannah says. "Bass is keeping the babies in the garage. He says any of them stupid enough to get close to him deserve to get eaten."

"Natural selection," Eugene says. "So, it's a *him?*"

"Well, I don't *know* that," Hannah says.

"You mean you haven't looked?"

"Anyway," she says, "I don't think he'd eat one of them."

"Oh, he'd eat one of them, all right. Catching them's the problem. I'd move the water dish to the other end of the cage. Make it safer for them. They're gonna come down in the night for water and he's gonna be waiting for them. Have himself a big supper."

"That's just it," Hannah says. "I can't get him to eat. Bass has had him for three days, and we haven't been able to get him to eat anything."

There are about seven crackers in the bottom of the cage. A couple pieces of toast. Two dog biscuits. A carrot. What looks like half a can of dog food. Some Gravy Train sprinkled in the water dish. A hard-boiled egg.

"I'll bet these birds are wondering what the hell's going on,"

Eugene says. "I've always heard they like chicken. Floating on water. Jesus, you ought to get him in some water, Mama. Y'all are gonna mess around and kill him."

Hannah tells Eugene that Bass and the Mexican were driving home after delivering a car when they saw the alligator in the road. They were in the Suburban, somewhere out around Gum Island. She tells him that when Bass jumped out the door, the vehicle still moving, the alligator took off for the rice fields. But that Bass caught it right before it reached a deep ditch by putting one foot on its tail, the other gently behind its head.

She tells him how they didn't have anything to put the alligator in so Bass told the Mexican to hold it, and the Mexican told Bass, "Bésame la cola!" And Bass told the Mexican to hold that alligator or walk the twelve miles back to town. And how the Mexican held it in the back seat in between his legs, holding its mouth shut with both hands. And how Bass laughed, and the Mexican cursed loudly in Spanish all the way into town.

"You're in your truck, aren't you?" Hannah says. "My husband has a whole parking lot full of cars, and I never have a thing to drive."

"Yes, ma'am," Eugene tells her. "The keys are in it."

"Let me get my purse," she says, walking up to the house.

Eugene is on his knees with his face pressed up against the chicken wire. He is looking through two holes that match up with his eyes.

Hannah walks back out to the cage, leaving the sliding glass door open. "Try these on him," she says, tossing a package of Oscar Mayers on the ground. "See if he'll eat some of those old wieners."

Toby walks out onto the patio. Toby is a fifteen-year-old Chihuahua. He's blind. Toby is just standing there, sniffing at the air, his head raised a little.

Hannah sees him, points, and says, "You better get your ass back inside."

Toby turns around and walks back toward the house. About halfway in the door, he stops and turns his head and listens.

"That's right, I'm talking to *you!*" Hannah says. "You stinky old dog."

Eugene says, "Is this thing even alive?"

"Sure he is," she says.

"How do you know? He eaten any of this stuff? I mean, he'll die if he doesn't eat. Look at his ribs. They ain't moving."

"His eyes are open," Hannah says.

"You can die with your eyes open, Mama." Eugene picks up the package of wieners. "Let's see if he'll eat some of these," he says.

"I'm going to hurry and run to the store," she tells him. She walks quickly up to the house. "*Chicken* is what I'm looking for?" she shouts from the patio.

"Chicken *necks!*" Eugene has opened the door and stepped inside the cage. "Get him some chicken necks!" he shouts up to her. The doves have all left their perches. They are flying around the top of the cage. Eugene squats down. He reaches over with a dead stalk of maize and taps the alligator between the eyes to see if he will blink. "You alive?" he says. The doves calm down again. He grabs the end of a wiener and holds it right up to the alligator's nose. "Are you?"

Eugene hears something behind him, near the door of the cage. He turns his head to see Toby trotting for the house with the package of wieners in his mouth. "Toby!" he says and just then feels something pull at his hand. He looks back to find nothing left of the wiener. He stands quickly, startling the doves, and stumbles backwards out of the cage. The doves' wings flapping about his ears. He is counting the fingers on his right hand.

"Mama?" he shouts at the house. "Hey Mama!" opening and closing his right hand. But he sees that she cannot hear him. She is backing down the drive in his truck on her way to the store.

Toby is on the patio, making little smacking sounds, eating Oscar Mayers.

HANNAH

BASS GETS up first in the mornings and puts on the coffee. Hannah is lying in bed with her eyes open. She is looking at a picture of her mother on the night stand. She jumps when she hears a gunshot from what sounds like the patio. She sits up in bed and listens. She hears another shot, farther off this time, like back in the yard, closer to the pasture. She gets out of bed and dresses quickly, pulling on her present from Eugene, a blue, short-sleeved Izod.

The glass door is open. Bass is out by the barbed wire fence, holding his .22 in one hand, looking down at something. Toby is out there with him. Hannah pours herself a cup of coffee and walks to the glass door.

Lately, something has been coming out of the pasture at night, killing the doves. Sometimes it tunnels under the cage. Sometimes it pulls the doves or what's left of them through the chicken wire. Maybe a coon or something. Lately, Bass has been keeping his rifle on the patio, close to the door.

"What is it?" Hannah shouts out at him. Bass reaches down and picks it up by the tail. "What is that?" she says. "A rat?"

"No, Hannah," Bass says. "It's a ostrich."

"I *know* it's a rat!" Hannah says. "I've just never seen one that big."

It is as large as Toby. Toby is standing on his hind legs, smelling of it.

"It's a *field* rat," Bass says. He swings it by the tail, over the barbed wire fence, into the pasture. "That's what's been killing the doves."

Toby walks under the fence, sniffing into the field.

Hannah is standing by the birdcage now. "What are we going to do with your little friend?" she says. She has placed Eugene's old twenty-gallon aquarium inside the cage. She has made a little walkway ramp up to the top of the aquarium, and the alligator is in there now, with only its eyes and nostrils sticking out of the water.

"Keep him awhile," Bass says.

"He'll outgrow this cage," Hannah says. "I mean, won't he?"

Bass is inspecting the chicken wire near the bottom of the cage to see if it is secure. "When he gets that big," he says, "I'll just have the people come out and dig us up a swimming pool for him." He looks at her. "Hell, Hannah, I don't plan on keeping him *that* long. I'll let him go soon enough."

"We're getting plenty low on birds," she says. "We had nineteen on my birthday. And now, we only have seventeen."

"I tell you the rats have been killing them!"

"But what if it ain't the rats? What if it's him? What if he's been eating all our doves?"

"You want me to kill him? Is that what you want?" Bass says, pointing the barrel of his rifle at the aquarium. "I can take him out and shoot him right now. I didn't know you hated the little fellow."

"Hush," Hannah says. "I don't hate him. I just want to bring my babies out to be with their Mamas is all."

"Soon," Bass tells her. He walks up to the patio and leans his rifle against the brick. He turns and looks at her. "Soon," he says.

Hannah bends down and looks at the alligator which is now lying at the bottom of the aquarium. The alligator in the aquarium looks at Hannah. She tells him, "Don't you go eating any more of my doves, you little bastard, or I'll have a pair of shoes made out of you."

HANNAH STANDS at the ironing board in the den. She is working on a pair of Eugene's Levi's. She is watching television at the same time. A man is telling a woman that he loves her. The woman is crying. The man asks the woman to trust him.

Hannah stops ironing. She says, "You trust that weasel, and you deserve to get hurt." The woman tells the man, "But I *do* trust you." Hannah tells the woman, "You're hopeless, honey."

Eugene opens the front door and says, "Knock, knock."

"Come on in," Hannah says. She walks quickly around the ironing board to turn off the television.

"Hey," Eugene says, "you don't have to turn your shows off."

"What?" Hannah says. "Those things? I don't waste my time watching those old shows. I'm just about done with your clothes," she says.

"No hurry," Eugene tells her. "I want to go out and check on your birthday present." He opens the glass door.

Hannah says, "He has a name now. It's Hannibal. Hannibal the Cannibal. He's been eating all our doves."

"I thought Daddy said y'all had a rat."

"We *had* a rat. Bass shot it. But it's that damn alligator that's been doing all the damage." Hannah stands the iron up. She turns the jeans over.

"You think?" Eugene says.

"I *know*," Hannah says. "I went out there this morning to feed him his dog food, and he had about ten white tail feathers sticking out of his mouth. He had this big grin on his face, too."

"Did he, now?"

"So I didn't feed him," Hannah says. "I didn't figure he needed feeding."

"I guess not," Eugene says. He's laughing. He closes the door behind him.

Hannah finishes the jeans. She folds them and unplugs her iron. She carries the ironing board into the utility room. She kicks at Toby and tells him, "Do you have to stay right under my feet, dog?" She gathers the rest of Eugene's clothes and places them carefully in his bag.

Eugene is back inside now.

Hannah tells him, "You'd better say good-bye to Hannibal. He's history." She lights a cigarette with a disposable lighter that fits into a tiny cowboy boot.

"What are y'all gonna do with him?"

"That's your daddy's department," she says. She blows her smoke away from him. "I told him either he gets rid of that alligator or I'm going to bring my birds inside."

Eugene says, "For Christmas, I thought I'd get you one of those little dog harnesses. You know, so you could walk old Hannibal down the road in the mornings."

Hannah just looks at him. "For Christmas," she says, "I think I'm going to get *you* a washing machine and an ironing board. When are you going to learn how to wash your own underwear, boy?"

"That's it," Eugene says. "You've hurt my feelings. I'm running away." He slings the duffel bag over his shoulder. "I'm running away, and I'm not ever coming back."

"Good," Hannah says.

Hannah sits in a lawn chair, next to the birdcage, listening to the doves. She is saying, "We're going to have to let you go pretty soon. You know that, don't you? Your Mama's probably out there somewhere wondering where you went." She is saying, "I'd keep you. I would. Except that you're eating all my babies. You don't know any better."

She is holding a tiny, bald dove in her lap. "Bass will take you off somewhere," she says. "Somewhere where you can be happy."

It is a Sunday morning. Bass has driven over to Old River to see his mother. Hannah is carrying baby doves one by one from the garage to the birdcage. Toby follows her back and forth each trip. Hannah places the babies on the front porch of the house of doves. She tells Toby, "You're not worth anything, are you?"

Hannah hears the telephone ring inside. She shoos Toby out of the cage. The phone rings again. "Coming!" she says, running up to the house. "Come on, Toby." She closes the glass door. "Hello!" she says, winded.

"Daddy done gone?" It is Eugene.

"Hi, Baby," she says. "Yeah, he left about an hour ago. For Grandma's."

"I was supposed to go with him," he says. "To help him mow."

Hannah is standing by the glass door. She is looking out into the pasture. There are two boys carrying BB guns walking in her direction. "He got tired of waiting on you," she says. "You know your father."

"Well, you tell him when he gets home that I've been out there trying to get my truck started for the last half hour," Eugene says. "You tell him that. He never did get my truck fixed!"

The two boys have climbed through the barbed wire fence. They are walking toward the birdcage.

"Hey," Eugene says, "you there?"

"I'll tell him," Hannah says. She is watching the boys, standing by the cage. She reaches and picks up Bass's .22 and taps the barrel on the glass so that the boys will look at her. She says, "Don't you even think about shooting one of those birds."

"What's that?" Eugene says.

"Nothing," Hannah says. "Some boys are out by the birdcage."

"Why don't you just sic old Hannibal on them?" Eugene says. He is laughing. "Just go out there and open the cage and say, 'Sic 'em, Hannibal! Sic 'em!'"

"Bass is letting him go this morning," Hannah says. She leans the .22 up against the wall. "Hold on a minute," she says to him. She places the receiver on the bar. She opens the glass door and shouts at the boys, "You'd better get the hell away from that cage, you hear!"

BASS IS in the habit of reading the Sunday morning paper Sunday evening when everything is quiet. He sits on the couch in the den and pushes the mute button on the television remote control and reads. Toby sits in the recliner.

Hannah washes the dishes that have accumulated over the weekend. She has a dishwasher, but this gives her something to do while Bass looks at his paper. They talk, sometimes. This reminds her of when Eugene was a little boy. She would set him on a barstool, and he would sit there quietly and watch her wash dishes. He would sit there until Bass called him over to read the funnies together.

"Where did you let him go?" Hannah says. She starts with washing the bowls, and then she works her way to the saucers, then the plates.

"The Number Three Road," Bass says. "Out by Mama's."

"Where?" Hannah says. She has her hot dishwater in the right side of the sink. She places washed bowls and saucers in the left side.

"Out by Mama's."

"I know," she says. "But where?"

"The Number Three Road," he says. He looks up from his paper. "By one of the canals. You know, where Gene and I used to go snake hunting."

Hannah is talking to him over the bar. "Did you put him in the water?" she says.

"No, I didn't put him in the water," he says. "I put him in the weeds next to the water. I'm reading the paper, Hannah."

"I know," she says. "But we can talk for a second." She is down to her plates. "I mean, did you put him close enough to the water so that he could find it if he needed to?"

"*Hannah,*" Bass says.

HANNAH DRIES her mother's silverware piece by piece. She places it in a drawer beneath the coffee maker. The knives are dry.

Bass is lying on the couch, asleep. Toby at his feet. The news is on. Hannah is listening. People are killed in the Middle East. People are killed in Central America. There is an oil spill in the Gulf. There are commercials.

When Hannah is finished, she folds her cup towel and places it on Eugene's barstool. She walks into the den, picks up Toby, and then sits in the recliner. She places Toby on his back in her lap, his head at her knees. She tickles him under the chin. Toby closes his eyes. She is leaning back in the chair, her shoes off.

On the television, they are talking about a new hunting season opening. They are showing men in boats shooting alligators in bayous and rivers. They are showing men pulling the large animals to shore with ropes.

"Hey," Hannah says. "What's that all about?" She nudges Bass's head with her foot.

"Huh?" he says. He is still asleep.

Hannah sits up. "Look!" she tells him. She shakes him by the shoulder. "What are they doing?" she says, pointing to the television.

"What?" Bass says. He slaps at her hand. "What!"

The Pope is on now. "You missed it," Hannah says. She lights a cigarette.

Bass sits up on the couch. He is rubbing his eyes with the heels of his hands. *"I'm listening,"* he says.

"I just saw that they're starting to hunt alligators," Hannah says. "That's all."

"There's an open season on them," he says. He gets his glasses from the coffee table. He looks at her. "The Oilers lose?"

"Why?" Hannah says.

"Why what?"

"Why did they just open the season on alligators?"

"There are too many of them," Bass says. "Their hide's expensive." He stands up. "I'm going to bed."

"But," she says. "But they wouldn't shoot our little Hannibal, would they?" She says, "I mean, for *his* skin?"

Bass has already walked out of the den and into the hallway.

"Would they?" Hannah shouts.

Bass sticks only his head around the corner. He has his eyes closed. "He's a baby, Hannah. He's a baby alligator," he says. "He ain't even four foot long. They don't shoot babies, Hannah." His head disappears around the corner. *"Good night,"* he says from the bedroom.

"Go on to bed, then," she shouts after him. "You grouchy old bastard!"

Hannah looks down at Toby. She is holding her cigarette with her lips. She grabs Toby's left front leg. Then she grabs his right front leg. She moves them back and forth quickly, like he's running. Toby growls and nips at her fingers. "I hate to tell you this, Toby," she says, "but your daddy is a mean old man."

Hannah wakes that night to Bass's snoring. She has her eyes open. She can hear the doves in the back yard, cooing, one to another. She had been dreaming.

Somehow, she was on the white shell Number Three Road out by Grandma's, and it was nighttime, and the rice fields were a green, almost black. The sky, a dark blue. She was standing on a bridge over one of the wide rice canals. The water wasn't moving. It was light brown in color, like chocolate milk.

She had been dreaming of that wide water, and in it was her birthday present, swimming away from her, toward the horizon, in a canal which had no end.

MARSH

MARSH!" she would shout. She would step from her bright kitchen onto her back porch at dusk and shout, "Marsh!"

And I would kneel down behind a large stone. I would hide in that fenced yard behind her house. I would stretch out on the cool grass, still hidden, and wait for him.

"Marshall!"

No lights in his dark house. No electricity.

First, I would hear the faint creak of his screen door. Then, I would see his white shirt in the twilight as he squinted into the dark yard. And if I listened carefully, I would hear his frail voice whisper my name.

"MARSH!" she said. She was on her knees in that yard behind her house. She was planting flowers.

I stopped running. "Yes, ma'am?" I said. I was chasing the dogs, or they were chasing me.

"Get those dogs outside the fence," she said, "and then come over here."

I started with a light dog. I started by saying, "Come here." I stooped over and picked him up and carried him out into her back yard. Each time, I kicked the gate closed behind me. And then I stooped over again and placed the little dog gingerly down on his legs. One by one, dog by dog.

The big dogs were too heavy to carry, so I had to reach down and lift them up by their front feet and walk them outside the fence. I had to walk backwards and lead them along slowly like I was pulling a wheelbarrow.

One by one, until the yard was empty, and the gate closed. "Good," I said, and all at once, dog by dog, they left me. They trotted off around the fence, back toward his house and some other game.

"Marsh," she said. She was standing now, and she was laughing.

"Yes, ma'am?" I said, and I didn't know how, but there they were, every last one of them, big dogs, little dogs, heavy and light, sitting with their mouths open, their tongues hanging out, smiling at me from the other side of the fence.

She pointed. "You're gonna have to close the back gate."

"Pretty flowers."

"Thank you," she said. She was holding a small shovel. "Do you like staying with me?"

"Yes, ma'am."

"I *think* you're old enough now," she said. "Listen, love, you shouldn't go running around in here. Do you understand?"

"No, ma'am."

She smiled. "This," she said. She followed the fence all the way around with her shovel. "This is your family."

"Oh," I said.

"Do you understand?"

"No, ma'am."

She said, "They are all buried here."

I looked off across the burnt orange carpet of pine needles at the bright white stones standing in rows. "Under the ground?"

"That's right," she said.

"Why?"

She just looked at me. "They've gone away, love. They're... dead."

"Oh."

She took me by the hand. "This," she said, pointing to the flowers. "This is my husband. Your grandfather. You look like him. You look like he looked when he was a little boy." She reached down and touched the stone. "Do you know what this says? Can you read it?"

"Reeve."

"That's right," she said. "And the other name? This one?"

"Marshall."

She smiled at me and squeezed my hand. "Do you know what that means?"

"No, ma'am."

She frowned and shook her head. "Look out, now!" she said, pulling me to her side. "Do you see how you're standing on them?"

"No, ma'am," I said, looking all around. "No, ma'am, I don't even *see* them!"

"Love, you can't *see* them," she said. "They're buried. Down in the ground." She placed her hand on the grass by the stone. "Here," she said. "Here is his head. His hands. Here, his feet. Do you see?"

I was looking beyond the yard. "Yes, ma'am," I told her. I was looking at his house.

"Come with me," she said, and we walked to a row of whiter stones. "These are my sons. Your uncles."

I was watching the dogs disappear underneath his house, and I knew.

"Are you listening to me?" she said. She was down on her knees, pulling the weeds around a small stone.

I knew what would happen next. I knew the screen door would open. I knew he would appear. "Kate?" I said.

And there he was, holding the screen door open as they, dog by dog, trailed out of his house, onto his front porch, down his front steps, into his front yard where they waited.

"Yes?" she said. "Here." She handed me a pot of dead flowers. They waited until they were all out, all down his steps, all sitting in his yard. They waited until he closed the screen door, and then, one by one, they disappeared under his house again.

"Who is that?"

"That's just Wick," she said. "He's your uncle. He's your great uncle."

"What's wrong with him?"

"Ain't nothing *wrong* with him," she said. "He's just old. He's just an old, old man. Don't you go bothering him."

"I won't," I said.

She pointed to the pot of flowers. "Take that up to the house for me."

"Yes, ma'am," I said and started walking for the front gate. Wick was already at his screen door again, and the dogs were already waiting.

"Marshall!" she shouted, and I almost dropped the pot of flowers. "Watch where you're going! You're walking all over them!"

And I stopped suddenly, still on the tips of my toes, afraid of taking one more step, and I looked around me, and for the first time, the entire yard was filled, elbow to elbow, with frowning relatives. "Kate?" I said over my shoulder. "Does it hurt?"

DEEP IN the night, the white stones glowed. I would lie awake on the verandah. I would sit up on my pallet and wait for them.

Out of the ground they came, just a few at first—to see if it was safe—and then the others followed, tiny lights rising up out of the earth until the yard was bright with them.

On they would shine and then *off,* disappear, on and off like slow hearts, reappear two stones down to talk with a brother, console a mother, search for a missing child.

Every morning, just about dawn, he would come in through the gate, walk about the yard, stop at each stone, and talk to them. And every morning, when the sun came up, all of them were gone, and there he was, standing in the middle of the yard, alone.

"MARSHALL!" she was shouting. She was inside Wick's house, and she was shouting, "Marshall!"

"Coming!" I said, running across the yard. "I'm coming!"

She was opening the screen door and letting the dogs out.

"Yes, ma'am?" I said, winded at the back gate.

"Come get these dogs!" she said. "And keep them out of the house!"

I hurried up to the porch, clapping my hands, shouting, "Get on!" I chased them down the steps. "Get on away from there!"

And as if they knew there was something wrong, they left the house, the porch, the front steps, and trotted over through the back gate and waited in the yard.

I was standing on the porch. I had never been inside.

She cracked the screen and handed me Lamar, a rat terrier, and said, "Stay out! Stay outside!"

And as the door closed, I squinted through the screen after her. I tried to follow her with my eyes into the dark house.

Where she stopped, there was a bed. There was someone in the bed, Wick. There were some things on the bed, sitting on the covers, dogs. She reached over and picked one up and carried it out to me.

"Here," she said, and when she opened the door, I looked past her, and my eyes caught something leaning up against the wall, next to the bed. It was a leg!

"You better run up to the station and get Mr. Charlie," she said. "You better hurry."

THEY CAME and carried Wick into the yard. They came to town and buried him. Family and friends, standing throughout the stones, dressed up, whispering, like at a Sunday service.

And when it was all over, the yard quiet, all my uncles walked back to Wick's house and sat on his porch, on his steps. All my uncles, old men then, sitting where they sat as boys, sitting where they listened to *their* uncle.

Wick had this leg, this artificial leg. It was hollow. It had a hole in it about three inches above the ankle.

On Sunday evenings, after supper, all my uncles, young boys then, would walk back through the yard with their coins. They would walk back through the gate and sit on his porch, on his steps. Each boy with money in his hand.

And Wick would wait for them. He would sit in his rocking chair and wait for them. He would slowly reach down and roll up his pants leg. And each boy, according to his age, would walk up the steps and deposit his coins into the hole in Wick's leg. And Wick would close his eyes and rock himself and tell them stories. He would tell them stories about their father, stories about Cuba. He would tell them stories about Daiquiri, Siboney, Las Guásimas.

MARSHALL AND Wick were horsemen. They were in San Antonio in 1898. They were sent by old man Phillips to purchase new horses.

The journey had been a long one, so Wick decided that they deserved a reward, so they celebrated. They spent that evening drinking, walking through the old Alamo, toasting Bowie, Crockett, Travis. Later that night, they returned to their hotel and threw a big party.

San Antonio was nervous with the news of the *Maine*. Everyone was talking of war.

"Them goddamn Mexicans!" someone said.

"Spaniards," someone said.

"Them goddamn Spaniards!"

Sometime around dawn, Wick counted their money, and most of it was gone. He tried explaining this to his brother, but Marshall was passed out on the floor under a poker table.

Should they wire Mr. Phillips for more money? Should they return with only some of the horses? Mr. Phillips would be angry either way, he would probably fire them, and it seemed a shame to end such a great party.

The doors of the saloon flew open. "We're at war!" someone shouted. "They're calling for volunteers!"

"Blowing up the goddamn *Maine!*" someone said.

"Just who do they think they are!"

"Remember the *Maine!*" someone shouted.

"Remember the Alamo!" someone shouted.

"What *is* the goddamn *Maine?*" someone said.

THERE *was* a call for volunteers. There was a call for horsemen, cavalrymen.

"Why not!" Wick told Marshall. "We've spent all our money!"

THE OLD AND THE LOST

"*Mr. Phillips's money,*" Marshall told Wick.

"We've spent all his money," Wick said, "and we can't go back without it."

"No, sir," Marshall said.

"They need volunteers for the cavalry," Wick said, "and we know horses."

"We *do* know horses," Marshall said.

"Why not!" Wick said. "Where are these bastards, anyway!"

"Cuba," someone said.

"*Let's go!*" Wick said. "Let's mount up and go!" Wick said. "Let's go *tonight!*"

"Cuba's a island," someone said.

"Then somebody'd better rustle us up a boat," Wick said. He staggered outside into the plaza and shouted, "Does anybody in this goddamn town have a boat!"

WICK WOULD just sit there, rocking in the dark. The boys listening until they were called home.

Marshall and Wick signed up. They volunteered. They met a Colonel Leonard Wood. They met a man by the name of Roosevelt. They were issued uniforms.

They were trained and drilled in camps outside San Antonio. They were shipped to Tampa where they were to wait for orders to sail to Cuba.

Wick told them about the arrival in Tampa, how they were nicknamed, "The Rough Riders."

They trained and waited, waited and trained. They waited to sail for over a month. And when the ships, the transports, finally arrived in Tampa Bay, there were not enough of them. There was a mad scramble to get aboard for fear of being left behind, for fear of missing the war.

Wick told them about the hardships aboard the transports, the serious overcrowding, the dark makeshift quarters in the holds. How they were assigned bunks, how they were ordered to just lie there for five days and wait for their orders to sail, how they were not allowed to stand up, to walk around, to stretch. And when those orders came, they had to stay down in those bunks in the holds of those ships another seven days until they reached Cuba.

WICK TOLD them that when the transports finally reached the waters south of Santiago, the horses were just dumped into the sea.

"The horses!" Marshall said. "They're just killing them! What're we gonna do!"

"Nothing," Wick said.

"Nothing!" Marshall said. *"They're just killing them!"*

"Yes, sir," Wick said, "they're just killing them. And before this is all over, they just might kill us too."

The horses were thrown overboard in the middle of the night, and because of their long confinement in the hot, dark holds, those that made it through the surf were in such poor shape they could not be used for most of the campaign. Most of the early charges and skirmishes were conducted on foot.

He told them about the landing at Daiquiri, the Spanish bonfires all along the shore, the fortified blockhouse high above the town. How their transport, the *Yucatán,* was the first to charge to shore to find the town abandoned, the blockhouse deserted. He told them about the march into Siboney, the skirmish at Las Guásimas, the march inland along the corduroy road.

Admiral Sampson had the entire Spanish fleet bottled up in Santiago harbor, and it was their job to march west from the beachhead. It was their job to take hill by hill, to take blockhouse by blockhouse, to take Santiago.

WICK TOLD them about the night before the great charge. How Roosevelt marched the Rough Riders to a small abandoned sugar plantation, how they fell in the next morning at dawn, how they watched the batteries of field guns pass them on the road.

The Rough Riders were to wait until General Lawton engaged the Spanish at El Caney, and then their orders were to charge and take the San Juan Heights.

In the distance, they could see a white blockhouse on top of a hill. Each man knew that the Spanish were dug in and ready, that the Spanish were waiting. Each man knew that this was it, the big battle, the last desperate defense of Santiago.

"This is it!" Wick told Marshall. "Stay close!"

Wick remembered the first barrage from the field guns of Grimes's battery, the Rough Riders cheering, the strange silence afterwards. He remembered the peculiar whistling in the air, louder and louder, and the next thing he knew, he was flat on his back, his legs blown out from under him. He remembered hearing someone shouting, "Let's go!"

And before he started feeling the pain, he said, "Wait a minute!" He said, "Tell them to wait a minute!" He tried to get to his feet, but he couldn't move his legs.

"Wick?" Marshall kept saying over and over. "Wick?"

Wick could hear people shouting, or were they screaming? Someone was holding him down, and someone was working on his legs.

Shells were landing all around them. "Get him out of here!" someone said.

Wick remembered Marshall and another man picking him up

and carrying him. "Doctor!" Marshall was shouting. "Where's the goddamn doctor!"

Wick heard someone say, "You better stop that bleeding!" so they put him down and wrapped his legs tighter.

All that Wick could think about was that his legs were on fire. "My legs are burning!" he said.

They picked him up again and carried him, sometimes walking, sometimes running, to the rear.

They were passing other wounded men, some limping, some hopping, some using their rifles as crutches.

A field hospital was set up at a ford in the Aguadores River. Most of the wounded were stretched out on the sandy bank, some limped into the water.

Wick was screaming now. "My legs are burning!" he said. "Put me in the river!"

"Where's the doctor!" Marshall was shouting.

"Ain't no doctor," someone said.

There were several men standing, sitting, lying in the river. There were several men bleeding.

There was a bluff above the field hospital. There was an officer standing on the bluff. "You men that ain't wounded," he was shouting, "we need you!"

Marshall lowered Wick into the river. The water now the exact color of blood.

A doctor waded out to them. "Get going," he told Marshall. "We'll take good care of him."

Wick was screaming, "Marshall!"

"Yes, sir?" Marshall said. "I'm here." He was holding Wick in his arms. He was cradling him.

"You!" the officer said.

"Coming!" Marshall said.

"Tourniquet!" the doctor shouted. He hurried up out of the river. "I need a tourniquet here!"

"Wick," Marshall said, "I got to get going."

"Don't," Wick said.

"I got to," Marshall said. "I'll be back. Don't you worry. They'll take good care of you."

The other man pulled Marshall up onto the bank.

"Marshall?" Wick said.

"I'll come back for you!" someone said.

Wick was by himself now. A man floated by facedown in the water. All that Wick could think about was that his legs were on fire. All that he could think about was getting deeper in the river. He pulled himself back with his arms. He pulled himself back in the red water until he was in the Channel, until the cool current caught him and carried him away.

"MARSH!" she said. She was standing at the front gate. The dogs were running around and around the inside of the fence, playing follow-the-leader. "Where are you?"

"Over here!" I told her. I was outside the fence, hidden by the wisteria. I was catching bees in a Mason jar.

I already had five jars of lightning bugs on the back porch, two to a jar, air holes punched in the tops. I only needed one more bee for my study to be complete. I was reaching conclusions:

Lightning bugs and bumblebees are about the same size.
They both have wings, and they can fly.

Lightning bugs shine in the dark.
Bumblebees do not.

Lightning bugs sleep during the day (I cannot find where) and fly at night (I think! But maybe it is too bright during the day to see them shine?).

Bumblebees sleep at night and fly during the day (I know because I have snuck out in the night and crawled under the wisteria and honeysuckle and have not heard them buzzing).

Lightning bugs will not shine as long as they know you are watching them.

Bumblebees will not shine if you are watching them or not (I have placed jars full of bumblebees around corners at night and peeked at them, behind trees, and they will not shine. But maybe they know that I'm secretly watching and shut themselves off. Maybe they shine bright yellow like fire when I am asleep!).

Bumblebees have teeth.
Lightning bugs do not.

Bumblebees are meaner than lightning bugs.

If you shake up a Mason jar full of ten lightning bugs for exactly sixty seconds and then screw off the lid and pour them out, they will all just fall on the ground and be dizzy for a while. And then, they will all slowly get to their feet and try to fly off (sometimes flying into a house or a tree).

If you try this with bumblebees, they will all fly out mad and chase you down and bite you all over the place.

"Marshall!" she shouted, and the bee bit me, and I screamed and dropped the jar.

"Yes, ma'am!" I said, shaking my hand.

She was pointing. "Go help your Uncle Wick," she said.

I looked over the wisteria, through the tall trunks of the loblollies, and there he was, standing on his front porch, holding on to a stanchion.

"Go get that from them!" she said.

I hurried around to where she was standing.

The dogs were running around and around the inside of the fence, and one of them was playing keep-away from the others. One of them—maybe it was Bowie—had something in his mouth, like an old bone, and he was running, and all the others were chasing after him trying to get it.

The front gate was open, and she was just standing there, waiting. "Go on, now!" she said. "Hurry!" She closed the gate behind me.

"What!" I said, and then I saw it. I saw what Bowie had in his mouth. I saw what the other dogs wanted. It was a leg! It was a part of a leg, from about the knee down. It even had a white sock on it and a little black shoe with the laces untied.

I looked over at Wick's place, and there he was, standing on his porch, holding himself up, looking hurt and betrayed. He even had his right pants leg rolled up to the knee.

Someone had run up on my great uncle Wick when he wasn't looking and stolen his leg right out from underneath him. And I couldn't decide if it was horrible or hilarious.

"Marshall!" She was standing on her back steps with her hands on her hips.

"*Yes, ma'am,*" I said. I looked off through the stones, and there they were, waiting on the far side of the yard, happy.

They were happy because they knew that they weren't supposed to be inside the fence. They were happy because they knew that I had come inside to chase them. They were happy because they knew that I could never catch them unless they wanted to be caught.

Marsh

I started out walking around the inside of the fence. I started out slowly at first, my hands in my pockets, my eyes on the grape clusters of wisteria, until I got closer to the back and started walking fast, faster, as fast as I could walk without running, until I reached the gate, grabbed it, slammed it shut, and shouted, "I got you now! You're trapped!"

And there they were, directly across from me, on the opposite side of the yard, back where I had started out, but it was okay, it was safe, because she had gone inside.

Crockett had it now, a quick collie, and I knew it was going to be some run, so I took off walking like I had before, slowly at first, eyeing them across the stones. Faster and faster I walked until I was at a slow jog and then a fast jog, faster, until I was at a slow run and then a sprint, one lap around the yard, two, until I had caught and passed Milam and Lamar, a crooked dachshund, a crippled terrier, and they ran with me for a while, until the other dogs, the entire pack, picked up the pace, four laps, five, and when I looked out front, when I looked out across the yard, I couldn't see any of them, and then I heard it, the barking, and I turned around, and there they were, all ten of them, all ten yards behind, except that now they were chasing *me.* Around and around the yard I ran, eight laps, nine, losing my lead on them, hounds at my heels, until I noticed Deaf Smith resting off to the side—the leg in his mouth—just standing there the whole time on top of one of my aunts.

And that was all that I could take. I didn't even stop running. I just collapsed. I just collapsed and lay there on the ground for a while until they all trotted back and started licking me in the face to revive me because they weren't even close to being tired. "Come on, come on, come on," they were saying, licking me in the face, "we aren't even close to being tired!" Ten dogs licking me in the face, afraid I might expire, until I couldn't even breathe, and I had to get on my hands and knees and crawl away from them and hide behind a tree.

"Enough!" I shouted, pulling myself to my feet, wiping all that dog spit off my face. *"I'm mad now!"*

This was Deaf Smith's cue. He took off into the stones, and they took off into the stones, and I took off after them.

Deaf Smith would dart around a stone and drop the leg, and Houston would be right there behind him and pick it up without breaking stride, so it was like a relay handoff except that they had an unfair advantage, and they knew it. They knew that they could run anywhere, but there I was. There I was chasing after them, losing ground, sidestepping, hurdling, avoiding my relatives.

Until finally, I just fell to my knees, exhausted. And one by one, they all circled back and sat around me, winded too a little, their mouths open, their tongues out. Dog by dog, they all circled back, until finally, Fannin appeared out of the stones and sauntered over and dropped the leg on the ground in front of me.

And I dove for it and grabbed it and hugged it. They were all just sitting there, looking at me.

And I leaped to my feet and held the leg up high over my head, expecting them at any second to start jumping for it, expecting an attack.

But they didn't. They didn't start jumping for it. They just sat there, looking at me, with sorrow in their eyes, sad that the game was finally over, truly, sincerely, genuinely sorry for what they had done.

"That's better!" I told them. "That's more like it!"

The leg was still in one piece. The leather straps looked pretty gnawed on. The white sock was pulled down below the heel. The little black shoe missing.

"You should be ashamed of yourself," I told them. And now, they weren't even looking at me. Now, they were all looking down at the ground. "That's right," I said. "You should be."

I adjusted the straps above the knee. I pulled the sock on, around the heel, up over the ankle. "There," I said, leaned back, hauled off, and threw the leg out over the stones, out across the yard, as far as I could throw it.

"Marshall!"

I was thinking about leaving it outside the back gate. I was thinking about just propping it up against the fence and then running back through the stones when she shouted, "Marsh, you're gonna have to hand it to him! He can't come down and get it!" I turned around and looked for her, but she had already gone back inside.

I took a few steps into his yard and stopped. The dogs had run under the house, and there they were, elbow to elbow, lined up, with only their heads sticking out, watching me.

Wick was still standing up on the porch. He was still waiting, so I lifted the leg and pointed at it and said, "Is this...yours?"

He reached out with his arm.

A few more steps. I glanced behind me. I had left the gate open on purpose. I wasn't about to hand the leg over to him until I saw if he was mean. I figured that no matter what happened, no matter how scared I got, I could still outrun a one-legged man.

He motioned with his hand. It meant, "Come closer."

I walked slowly to his front steps and stopped. I was holding the leg behind me.

"Come on," he said. "Come on up here." He turned and hopped over to an old rocking chair and plopped down into it. The whole porch shook. "Ain't gonna bite you," he said. "Ain't got no teeth!"

One step, two steps, three, until I could see that the porch had just about rotted through. Just about every other board was missing. Wick's rocking chair had wedged itself down into one of these cracks. He couldn't have rocked if he'd wanted to. Any day now, Wick's rocking chair was going to fall right through the porch.

"I've seen you before," he said, his voice a whisper. He pointed with something that looked more like a bone than a finger. "Out there."

Kate was right. Wick *was* an old, old man. He was skinny like a skeleton. He hardly had any skin on him at all. And what he did have, I could see through. I could see blue blood vessels. I could see red veins crossing and crisscrossing all over him like the paths and trails of an old treasure map.

"Here," he said, and I slowly placed the leg in his hand, and he started strapping it on. He was strapping it on without even watching what he was doing. He was watching me. He was just sitting there, staring at me. "Who are you?" he said.

"I'm Marshall," I told him.

He stopped what he was doing. He didn't even roll his pants leg down. "Marshall?" he said.

"Yes, sir?"

He shook his head. "You ain't Marsh," he said.

"Yes, sir," I told him, "I am. That's my name. Marsh."

He motioned with his hand. "Come over here," he said, "where I can see you."

I looked off the porch, across the yard, to her house. "I should be getting back."

"Here," he said. He patted the top of his good knee. "Over here by me."

I stepped carefully over the missing boards and stopped right in front of him.

It was almost dark. It was almost suppertime. Any second now, Kate would call my name and save me.

Wick slowly reached out with a crooked finger and touched me just under the chin and tilted my head back a little. He squinted at me like he was trying to read my face. "Marsh," he whispered, "is that you?"

"Yes, sir," I told him, "it's me."

He frowned at me. "I thought you was dead," he said. He was shaking his head. He was just sitting there with one shoe on, one shoe off, staring past me now, out over the yard. "No," he said. "No, I coulda swore...Are you sure?"

"Yes, sir," I said. I had to think about it. "Pretty sure."

He smiled. "I knew it," he said. He pointed to the yard. "I saw you out there, and I just knew it."

And I was smiling too. "It's me," I told him.

"I've been waiting," he said. "I've just been...waiting."

"Here I am," I told him.

"Where you been?" he said. And then he said, "Is this it?"

"Sir?"

"This," he said. "Is this...it?"

And I didn't know what to say, so I said, "I think so."

"Good," he said. "Good." He was looking past me now. He was looking past the porch, over the fence, into the yard. "I've been thinking," he told me. "I don't sleep anymore. I've been thinking about Bloody Ford, the shallow place in the river."

And then I heard her and didn't want to. I heard her shout, "Marsh!"

"I've been thinking about you lowering me into the water," he said. "The river as red as blood." He was far away now. He was far away, somewhere else.

"Marshall!"

"I got to get going," I told him.

"And you said, 'I'll be back. Don't you worry.' "

I started for the steps and stopped. "I'll be back," I told him. "Don't you worry."

"And you said, 'I'll come back for you.' "

"Marshall!"

He looked at me and smiled. "Go on, now," he said. "She's calling. She does that. She misses you."

SHOOTING STARS

SUMMER, PAST midnight. The windows are open. A scratch at the screen.

"Listen," I whisper, shake her softly by the shoulder. "Sweetheart, it's time."

"Really?" she says. She's suddenly awake. She sits up in bed. "Well then, let's go!"

The scratching becomes a soft rapping on the wooden screen frame. I hurry over. Any second it will wake our mother. I can see him outside, standing there in his jeans, slumped, no shirt, holding a rifle. "We're coming," I whisper. It must be a clear night.

I help her on with her slippers. Little rabbits Mama made of cloth. The head at her toes, a cotton nose. The long ears stick out on both sides of the shoe.

I unlatch the screen, lift and set her on the sill. He has already propped his rifle against the house, and when I push the bottom of the rusty screen out, he reaches in and takes her.

"Careful," I tell him.

She looks over her shoulder, frowning. She reaches back for me. "*My* . . . ," she says too loudly, and they are gone hand in hand into the darkness.

I grab her sock filled with pennies from the night stand and crawl backwards through the window, bumping the screen open with my bottom.

They are to the road by now, so I run after them, in my pajamas, barefooted through the night.

No one is awake at this hour. No porch lights. There is no
moon.

Deep in the Thicket, there are few places, if any sometimes, to
see the sky. The road is the only paved passageway through this
wood. There are places where the trees grow together overhead
to form a dark tunnel for miles.

But here, on both sides, there are loblolly pines, high, a good
strip of sky. This is where I find them. He, with his back turned,
loading the rifle. She, off to one side.

It has always amazed me how the blacktop holds its heat
through the night. Impossible to cross barefooted at noon. It is
warm now under my feet, soporific. On chilly nights, after heavy
rains, the animals of the Thicket hop, slither, crawl out of the cold
marshes onto this road, stretch out on it, dry, warm as a mother's
side, and sleep until a car comes along.

She beckons with her hand. It means, "Hurry." Little prints
of sleeping rabbits on her pajamas. Little sister.

She takes the sock of coins and hands it to the quiet one. She
is wide-awake now, so proud of herself.

He tucks the rifle under his arm, empties the sock into his
palm and shakes that hand up and down to hear the sound of the
coins in the dark. He pours them into his pocket, lifts the rifle
above his head and points it at the sky.

Now it is my turn as intermediary to pick her up and show
her the stars.

She is to select one, not a big star because it would not be fair.
I am to tell the quiet one which star she has chosen. He will aim
his rifle, take time aiming, seconds, minutes, and then shoot
that burning orb from the sky. It will fall, plummet, race straight

down to the earth, Western Hemisphere, North America, East Texas, Big Thicket, strike the asphalt some half mile away, explode (not loudly, for it is a tiny star) and then burn itself out in the darkness.

"Aww," she will say. This is what pains me. She will look so sad. She will start running down the blacktop for the fallen star which is now just a tiny fire disappearing in the distance. She will not get there in time.

"Aww," she will say like the day she held her Easter chick in her hands and watched it die.

How can I tell her about these things? How can I tell her it is not true when she wants to believe so badly? How can I tell her that what he loads and fires, the projectile, is a wee wooden arrow, kitchen match, three inches long, propelled by a small metal sphere, pushed down the barrel high in the sky up to that point where something in the earth calls it back–that it then falls, plunges, red head first, white-eyed, quite a ways, so that when it strikes the pavement, it strikes and burns a dying fire down the dark road?

One of her slippers falls to the blacktop. "I'll get it," I tell her, stoop and grab the rabbit by the ears.

We are both staring straight up out of the Thicket. I raise my hand to show her.... The night is a black beast, a winged thing, with a thousand eyes.

Will I have the time to one day tell her that this star, a star we see one night, went out, is dead, died a long time ago–there is no more fire? How does it go? That it has taken all this time for the light to get to us. Something like that. So that what we are seeing, little sister, is like a memory of someone who has passed away.

No, tonight she is mine. I reach and pick her up. I hold her to me closely.

The quiet one rests the rifle on his shoulder.

"Mmm," she says, indecisive. She is holding her forefinger to her lips. And then she sees it. "There," she says. She points between the peaks of pines.

"You sure?" I ask her. I want it to be perfect. I want her to be happy. It is a tiny star, not really red, not yellow, but pink, winking off and on.

"That's it," she whispers. She has her arm around my neck. She gently pulls my head to hers so I can look down her short finger to the sky. She whispers, "That's the one."

◆◆◆◆◆◆◆◆◆◆◆◆◆◆◆◆◆◆◆◆◆◆◆◆◆◆◆◆◆

THE OLD AND THE LOST

For Logan Delano Browning

I WAS BORN in a land of bayous, raised between rivers. There is a place in Southeast Texas where two rivers meet and become one. There is a long bridge over these waters, and as you drive across, you can look to the south and see where the Old River and the Lost River become the Old and the Lost. You can look out as far as you can see and watch this wide water become the bay.

There is a small town just north of this bridge where my father and his father were born. My father and his brothers were raised between these rivers. His brothers, my uncles, were older, and both of them left without teaching him to swim.

When the Japanese attacked Pearl Harbor, my father and his brothers joined the armed services. One joined the Air Force, and one joined the Army, and because my father was the youngest, and because he was determined to be his own man, he joined the Navy. There was a small problem. My father was afraid of the water. The Navy tried and tried to teach him to swim—ordered him to dive off the decks of ships, ordered him to jump out of tall towers—but he couldn't learn, so they stuck him in the *Segundo*—they stuck him in a submarine—and when he reminded them that he couldn't swim, they told him not to worry. They told him not to worry about it. They told him that if anything happened way down there, he wouldn't *need* to swim. They told him that if anything happened down there at the bottom of the ocean, he'd be dead anyway.

WHEN I heard about the hurricane, I called the airport to book a flight, and they asked me if I was crazy. They asked me if I was insane, so I jumped in my truck and headed south. Through Virginia and Tennessee. Through Mississippi and Louisiana. Twenty-four hours. Back to Texas. Down the old highway. Orange. Beaumont. China. Nome. Past pasture after pasture. Past abandoned airstrips. Closed cattle auctions. Devers. Raywood. Ames. Past rice field after rice field where the farmers went broke. Past soybean field after soybean field where the farmers went broke. Past Brahma bulls. Billboards stripped bare by the storm. Deserted dryers. The elevators where they stored their grain. The tall, white towers like castles of the late King Rice until the king died, and the workers moved away, and the fields lay fallow up and down the highway.

I drive across the Old and the Lost and back to Sour Lake. I drive down Main Street, around the courthouse, around the square, and think of the Hoffmans. And then I drive to the end of the road.

THIS IS what I remember. I remember a big house with columns, a long lawn lined with live oaks, a driveway that ran up under the porch. I remember the low limbs of the live oaks, the hanging Spanish moss that hid the house from the road. And I remember the family.

The father and the mother owned stores on the square. The father sold expensive suits to Southern gentlemen. The mother sold pretty dresses to Southern ladies. His store was on one side of the courthouse. Her store was on the other side. My father and my mother did not shop at these stores.

What I remember about the parents is that they were always dressed up. The father always wore a coat and tie—even in the summer—a different suit every day. The mother always wore pretty dresses. My mother said that was easy when you owned the store. My mother said that if she owned the store, she'd wear pretty dresses too. Even the old Negro wore a bow tie.

What I remember about the family is that they were always smiling. The father. The mother. The little girl with the thick black hair. The little boy with the thick glasses. My mother said that was because they had money. They had the nicest house, they wore the nicest clothes, and they were smiling. People were always asking me what I wanted to be when I grew up, and when they'd ask me, I'd tell them, "When I grow up, I want to be happy." Of course, everybody hated the Hoffmans. But to me, as a small boy, in a small town, they were the royalty. They were the king and queen of Sour Lake. Every Saturday, I would follow them from a distance as they walked downtown to the depot, and every Saturday, I would wait on the platform for the train which would take them to their special church in Houston.

I remember climbing the low limbs of the live oaks and watching the children play. A little girl and a little boy. Grayson and Gregory. She wore braces on her teeth. He wore braces on his legs.

Every Sunday afternoon, they played on the long lawn. The old Negro carried the set from the garage. He stuck stakes in the ground. He stuck a stake at one end of the yard, and then he stuck a stake at the other end. The stakes were painted with pretty stripes. Blue. Red. Black. Yellow. Green. Orange. He stuck these white hoops into the ground. He made measurements. He positioned them carefully. Some on this side of the yard. Some on the other side. He brought out the picnic table and the chairs and placed them under the live oaks. He brought out a great big pitcher of tea.

And then the front door flew open, and then the little girl ran out, with her long black hair, with her bright red bows. The mother right behind her, laughing onto the lawn. And there was the little boy, holding onto the door frame, walking out on his stiff legs. The father standing behind him to catch him if he fell. The two of them wearing the same striped coats, the same striped trousers, which looked more like pajamas than Sunday school clothes.

The old Negro walked out onto the lawn. He handed the children their long wooden hammers. He handed them their painted wooden balls. The little girl was always red. The little boy was always blue. The father and the mother sat down in their chairs. The old Negro poured the tea, and then the children started. They hit their balls. They started at the stake at one end of the yard and ended at the stake at the other end. They hit their balls through the hoops. They took turns. The little girl, shrieking, running across the lawn, swinging her hammer between her legs. The little boy, hobbling to the next hoop—the head under his arm—using his hammer like a crutch. The old Negro, "Some more tea, Ma'am?" The mother, "Please." The father, "Thank you." *Smack*, the little girl slapping her ball across the lawn. *Tap*, the little boy shuffling along behind her. The little girl screaming when she cleared a hoop. The little boy knowing he would never catch her. The mother, "Grayson, slow down a little, Sweetheart." The father, "Gregory, you're doing just fine, Son." Until finally, invariably, the red wooden ball rolled up against the blue wooden ball. The little girl cheered. The little boy frowned. The mother, "Sweetheart?" The father, "Don't." The old Negro, "Miss Grayson, you be nice, now." But before he could replace his pitcher, before the parents could rise from their chairs, the little girl placed her bright red shoe on her red wooden ball and sent the blue wooden ball sailing into the trees. The mother, *"Grayson."* The father, *"Let him get it."* The little boy, without pouting, without complaining, limped off into the live oaks. The little boy disappeared into the Spanish moss.

The sun was going down. It was getting dark. The little girl cleared another hoop and cheered. The father and the mother watched the trees. The mother took his arm. The father took her hand. There was no breeze. There was no movement in the moss. The pocket watch ticking in his jacket. The ice cubes settling in their glasses. The mourning doves cooing in the dusk.

The old Negro dropped the pitcher of tea. "Mister Gregory!" he shouted. He started running across the lawn. He stopped at the low limbs of the live oaks. He parted the thick drapes of the Spanish moss and said, "Mister Gregory?"

I STAND on this lawn fifty years later. There are no croquet wickets now. No wooden mallets. No painted balls. There are only wheelchairs and walkers scattered across the yard. There are school buses up and down the driveway. An ambulance parked underneath the portico.

Early Classical Revival. Four Doric columns. The twin side wings were added after the Revolution. The Texas Revolution. What were they thinking? Too big of a house for the Hoffmans. The builders, the first family, were not farmers. They did not sow the rice. They did not harvest the rice. They did not own the fields. They owned the canals, and they owned the water in the canals. They dug these ditches to the Old and the Lost and provided irrigation to those who could pay. My grandfather rode these levees on horseback. He monitored the gates for the men who sold these rivers. He made meticulous measurements. One quarter of an inch. One eighth of an inch. One sixteenth of an inch of water.

I have memorized this mansion. The storm shutters stripped away. The windows shattered. The pediment plastered with leaves. I walk across the lawn. I see the water line on the columns. The dirty rings of debris. The tidal surge must have been ten feet high. The azaleas killed by the salt water. The ambulance submerged.

The same front door. The same lion-faced knocker. I step inside. Two firemen splash past me and disappear into the darkness. The foyer is underwater. One inch, maybe two. I hear the groaning of the generators. I hear the humming of the box fans. I hear someone shouting, "We need somebody to run into town!" The foyer smells like salt water, dead fish, and urine. A black orderly with a push broom sweeps the water outside. I hear someone shouting, "We need somebody to get us some gas!" There is a reception desk, and there is another push broom propped up against it. There is a wall of filing cabinets. Their drawers open. Their files missing.

A police officer walks up behind me. "You work here?" he says.

"No," I say.

"Then get the fuck out of the way," he says.

I turn to face him, eye to eye.

"*Please*," he says and shoulders past. "Who needs the hearse!"

A large black woman shouts from the landing, "Get rid of that water!"

"Yes Ma'am," the orderly says.

"Can you help me!" I shout over the sound of the sweeping.

"I doubt it!" she shouts back.

"I'm looking for someone," I say.

"Good luck!" she says. She's holding a clipboard. She's wearing a white dress. White stockings. She starts storming down the stairs. "Where's Daunte!" she shouts.

"Taking his break," the orderly says. He looks like he's getting ready to run.

She walks up to him through the water. She swats him with the clipboard. "Go get his ass," she says, "and tell him there ain't no more breaks!" She drops the clipboard on the desk. "Give me that!" she says and snatches his broom. She starts sweeping. "You gone stand there," she says without looking at me, "you gone get wet!"

I step out of her way. "I was hoping you could help me," I say.

"Honey," she says, "we're *long* on hope around here." She pushes the water through the front door. "But we're mighty *short* on help."

"What happened?" I say. "The lake get up?"

"Do what?" she says. She slaps the push broom on the steps.

"All this water," I say. "Did the lake get up?"

She stops sweeping. She just looks at me. "What's wrong with you?" she says.

"Pardon me?" I say.

She walks back to the base of the stairs. "Did the lake get up!" she says. She starts sweeping. "The lake *don't* get up," she says. "The lake *can't* get up. It's a lake!"

"But all this?" I say. "All this water?"

"Every now and then," she says, "them rivers bleed together and drown this whole country."

"The storm," I say. "Didn't the hurricane come up in here?"

She stops sweeping. "Where you from?" she says.

"Here," I say.

"Here?" she says.

"Sour Lake," I say.

"I doubt it," she says. "We don't tolerate no stupid children. You musta been adopted." She grabs the other push broom. "Till he gets back, you get to be Daunte," she says. "You two could be related."

I show her my cup. "Do you have someplace I can put this?" I say.

She nods to the desk. "What is it?" she says.

"A milk shake," I say.

"Where'd you get that?" she says. "Who's got electricity?"

"Beaumont," I say.

"Beaumont," she says. "Beaumont's got electricity."

"Can I put this someplace?" I say. "Someplace cold."

"What're you asking me?" she says. "Do I got a icebox?"

"Do you have an icebox?" I say.

"I gotta bunch of iceboxes!" she says.

"But not for me," I say. "Not for *my* milk shake."

"Not for *nobody's* milk shake!" she says. "We don't got electricity! We don't got water! We don't got gas! You understand?"

"I understand," I say.

"Even if we *had* electricity," she says, "we can't go storing somebody's milk shake! We got supplies. We got treatments. We got medications for our residents." She reaches for the cup. "I say we split it," she says, "before it melts."

I set the milk shake on the desk. "It's not for me," I say. "It's not mine to share."

She hands me the broom.

"Where's your help?" I say.

"You're it," she says, and we push the rivers back outside. We sweep the white tile clean, and before we can move our brooms, the dark water covers it again.

I look around the foyer. "Where is this coming from?" I say.

"The rivers, the bay, the Gulf of Mexico," she says. "Pick."

"Did you leave?" I say.

"We wanted to leave," she says. "We needed to leave. We called and we called, but nobody came. The police department didn't come for us. The fire department didn't come. And then we lost our electricity. And then we lost our phones."

We slap our brooms under the portico. "Everybody was at Happy Valley," she says. "Everybody was at the golf course. The police and the fire department. Rich people don't like to get wet!"

"Did they evacuate you?" I say.

"Not till they got everyone else," she says. "The country club got police cars and fire trucks and ambulances. We got school buses."

We slosh through the foyer. "We're not doing any good," I say.

"You're lucky you ain't working for me," she says.

"Why's that?" I say.

"I'd fire your whiny ass!" she says.

"What about your patients?" I say. "What about your residents?"

"We took them where we could," she says. "All the way up 105 to Cut and Shoot. We dropped them off where there was room. Saratoga. Batson. Moss Hill. Cleveland. When we got to 45, the interstate was a parking lot. Bumper to bumper. Galveston to Dallas. Three hundred miles. One terrified traffic jam. Nobody moving. Nowhere to go. One hundred degrees. One hundred ten. We just sat there and cooked. No air conditioning. Everyone ran out of water. Everyone ran out of gas. People lost their dogs on that hot highway. People lost their children. We lost six of our residents in them school buses. And then the sun went down, and the storm came in, and we closed up our windows and just sat there in the dark while that hurricane kicked the hell out of us."

We start sweeping.

"It sounds like you did what you could," I say.

"We saved who we could," she says. "We got the rest upcountry."

"Did you go back for them?" I say.

"We ran out of gas," she says. "Everybody ran out of gas. *The gas stations ran out of gas*."

"But after the hurricane?" I say. "After the storm?"

"We didn't know where to look," she says.

I stop sweeping. "You didn't keep records!" I say. "You didn't keep track!"

She slaps her broom on the steps. "We were running from this water!" she says. "We were racing that storm! Did we keep track! We kept them old folks out of harm's way! We found safe harbors for all but the six! We held their hands through the hurricane!" She props her broom against the house. "We fanned them all day," she says. "We sang hymns all night. We prayed all the way through the storm. We just sat in them school buses and watched them die."

We hear them laughing before we see them. They are walking up the driveway. When they see us, they toss their cigarettes into the azaleas.

She shakes her head. "Daunte," she says.

"Yes Ma'am," Daunte says.

"You are one worthless nigger," she says.

"I know, Mama," Daunte says.

She hands her push broom to the orderly. I hand mine to

Daunte. "Get to sweeping," she says. "Push them rivers back to the bay."

She grabs her clipboard, I grab my milk shake, and we step out under the portico.

"Why don't you let me drink that," she says, "before you go and melt it!"

The sun is going down, and what is left is streaming through the hanging Spanish moss.

"I'm looking for someone," I say.

She shows me the clipboard. "Does this someone have a name?" she says.

"Fannin," I say. "James Walker Fannin. He's my father."

"Fannin," she says. "Mr. Fannin. I remember Mr. Fannin."

"Do you have him?" I say. "Is he here?"

"Oh, Honey," she says, "I couldn't tell you."

"You can't tell me?" I say. "You don't know?"

"I don't know *who* we got," she says. "What I *know* is this. Who we got is safe and sound. Who we got is high and dry."

I point at the clipboard. "Is he on there?" I say.

"Maybe," she says. "Maybe not." She lifts the clipboard. "But this," she says, "don't mean nothing! This don't mean a thing!"

"Mama," Daunte says, "this old water must be up in these walls!"

"Shut up and sweep!" she says.

"Was he here?" I say. *"Was he on the buses?"*

"If he was here," she says, "he was on the buses."

I point at the clipboard. "May I see that?" I say.

"Help yourself," she says. "We got them babies all over the place. At other hospitals. At other homes. We got old folks now we didn't have then. They got dropped off. They got deposited. No identification! No papers! We don't even know their names!"

She looks out over the lawn. *"Daunte!"* she shouts. *"Goddamnit to hell!"* She starts jogging across the yard.

"Yes Ma'am?" Daunte says. He steps outside.

"Help me!" she shouts. I look out across the lawn. The walkers. The wheelchairs, and in one of them, a frail body slumped over the side.

"Pratt!" Daunte says. He starts running, still holding his broom. The orderly steps outside, and the two of us start running. We catch up with her, and we all reach the wheelchair together. "Miss Bernadette," she says, "where you been?"

Miss Bernadette is just sitting there, staring straight ahead. She looks like she has been waiting underwater.

"Pratt," she says, "take her inside."

"Yes Ma'am," Pratt says. He scoops up Miss Bernadette and cradles her in his arms.

"Daunte," she says, "take her chair."

"Yes Mama," Daunte says, and we all walk across the yard.

I scour the clipboard for my father.

When we reach the portico, she says, "I'm gonna need that back."

I point to a name that has been crossed off with magic marker.

"I didn't do that," she says.

"What does it mean?" I say.

"Nothing good," she says.

Pratt starts up the stairs with Miss Bernadette. Daunte starts sweeping.

"Listen, Honey," she says, "I hope you find him, but I got my hands full." She steps behind the desk. She opens a drawer. "Whoever we got," she says, "we got upstairs. We had to move them up out of the water just in case the city turns the juice on." She hands me a flashlight. "You're welcome to look," she says.

She walks down the hallway and disappears into the darkness. "But you're on your own."

"Don't I know it," I say.

I climb the steps to the landing. They have installed a gate to keep the residents from falling down the stairs. I shine the flashlight to the right and to the left, to the east and to the west, down the dark hall.

Pratt emerges with Miss Bernadette. "No beds," he says.

I open the gate for him, and then I step through.

"Daunte," he says, "where you want her?"

I start down the hallway. An elderly woman appears before me. She is wearing a muddy nightgown. She is wearing her white hair past her shoulders. She grabs my arms with her long nails. "Charlie?" she says.

"No Ma'am," I say.

She releases me and shuffles away.

The walls of the hallway are lined with wheelchairs. Most of the residents have straps across their chests to keep them from falling over. Some blink when I shine the flashlight in their eyes. Some do not blink.

I stop at each door and step inside.

"Margaret?" a man says.

I shine my light on him. He is sitting on the bed with his legs over the side. He is barefooted. He is wearing pajamas. "Margaret," he says, "is that you?"

"No Sir," I say and walk away.

Someone touches my arm in the darkness. "Is it over?" she says. "Is it coming back?"

"It's over," I say. There is a train of wheelchairs behind me.

"Are we leaving?" someone says.

"Not yet," I say.

The names on the doors have been crossed off, and other names have been written on the doors. Someone has drawn question marks with magic markers.

There is a room decorated with antique cars.

There is a room decorated with angels.

There are box fans in the windows. Extension cords to the generators.

I hear her downstairs. "Daunte!" she shouts.

"Yes Ma'am!" Daunte shouts.

"We need somebody to run into town!" she shouts. "We need somebody to get us some gas!"

An old gentleman greets me in a coat and tie. He is weaving over his walker. "Are you looking for Mr. Milam?" he says.

"No, thank you," I say, and he hobbles away.

I step into a quiet room. "Daddy?" I whisper.

"Not here," a frail voice replies.

I walk to the end of the hall. The room is dark. The drapes drawn. There are picture frames resting on the floor. Photographs leaning up against the wall. I shine the flashlight on each one of them. My father's father. His brothers. His *Segundo*.

I step inside. "Daddy?" I say.

He's lying on his side, facing the fan, his back to me.

I clear my throat.

There is a chair by the door for the breeze. The milk shake has melted, so I sit and find the straw.

I hear something out back. The generators start to stutter.

"Hey!" someone shouts down the hallway.

The box fan begins to die.

"Generators down!" someone shouts.

"Goddamnit!" she shouts. "Goddamnit to hell!"

I hear everything now. The creaking of the wheelchairs. The

rubber stoppers of the walkers. "I'm ready," someone says. The wheezing. The heavy breathing. "Mr. Milam?" someone whispers.

"No," I whisper. "Sorry."

A collective sigh through this silence.

He turns in his bed. He rolls onto his back and groans.

I can't see him in the darkness. I can only see his silhouette. "Sure is a lot of groaning over there," I say.

"I got a whole hell of a lot to groan about," he says and starts coughing.

"Want me to get you some water?" I say.

"I don't want to see no water again!" he says.

"I don't doubt it," I say.

"How long you been here?" he says.

"Thirty minutes," I say. "Maybe an hour. Your milk shake melted, so I drank it."

"Help yourself," he says.

"I done did," I say. "It's gone."

He starts again. He sounds like he's coughing up his lungs. He's trying to get up on his pillow. He's trying to prop himself up.

I stand and start across the room.

He points. "Sit!" he says. His voice hoarse.

"You all right?" I say. "You don't *sound* like yourself."

He tries to clear his throat. "I don't *feel* like myself," he says.

"Want me to call you a nurse?" I say. "Want me to call you a doctor?"

"There ain't no nurses round here," he says. "There ain't no doctors. They all got sent to Galveston." He pulls back the drapes and spits out the window. "I don't guess we're worth saving."

I hear something behind me. I turn and find an old man standing in the doorway. He's leaning forward. He's holding a cane in each hand. He looks like he's been swimming in his nightshirt. "Mr. Milam?" he whispers.

"No!" I say and shoo him away. I look back to the bed. I squint through the darkness. "You sick?" I say.

"I just got the crud," he says.

"What all's wrong with you?" I say.

"I don't know," he says. "*They* don't know. They thought it was a stroke. They thought it was Parkinson's. And now they think it's MSA."

"Multiple sclerosis?" I say.

"Atrophy," he says. "Multiple Systems."

"Atrophy?" I say.

"Multiple Systems Atrophy," he says.

"Do I want to know what that means?" I say.

"Piece by piece," he says, "part by part, God's shutting my ass down."

"He does that," I say.

"He's been after me my whole damned life!" he says.

"He found you," I say.

"Multiple Systems Atrophy," he says. "It's just a fancy way of saying I'm dying."

"When'd you get back here?" I say.

"I couldn't tell you where 'back here' is," he says.

"Sour Lake," I say.

"Sour Lake," he says. "Why the hell not! Another backwater!"

"Beats being swept out to sea!" I say.

"I wonder," he says. "I wonder. They should've wheeled me out to the end of a pier. They should've chained my chair to a live oak tree. They should've let that storm come in here and take me." He pulls back the drapes and looks outside. "Sour Lake," he says. "Dead can't be no worse than this!"

"Where'd you think you were?" I say.

"Ever since the storm," he says, "I been in church houses, hospitals, high school gyms. I been in rest homes, nursing homes, old folks' homes. I been in police cars, fire trucks, school buses. I shit you not—I couldn't tell you what state I'm in!"

"But they came for you," I say. "They got you out."

"Not for a while," he says. "Not for a while. They let us wriggle. They let us writhe."

"I heard about the buses," I say. "I heard about the highway."

"We just sat in our rooms and watched our televisions," he says. "We watched the hurricane leave the Atlantic, come into the Caribbean, move into the Gulf. The Leewards. The Windwards. The Greater Antilles. We heard that it was a big storm, a mean monster, a category three. The reporters said that there would be a surge. The reporters said that we should get the hell out. The reporters said that if we didn't get out, we wouldn't get out. The ferries would be shut down. The drawbridges closed. The evacuation routes flooded. We just sat in our rooms and watched our televisions."

"Two hundred," he says. "One hundred. Fifty miles out. And then the storm stopped. It just stopped. It just sat out there and strengthened. Category four. Category five. It crept up and down the coast. And we just sat there. We just sat there and waited. This was the day before landfall. This was the night before they came for us. And then the storm started coming in, and the lights started going out, and everyone started screaming."

"But they evacuated you," I say.

"Not for a while," he says. "They herded us into the hallway. They rolled us in our wheelchairs. They rolled us in our beds. They crammed us in like cattle in a car. The wind was blowing. The windows were breaking. They closed the doors up and down the hallway, and we just sat there in the dark and waited. Everyone was screaming and shouting. Everyone was crying and praying. And when those buses came, they piggybacked us out through the night. They carried us in their arms like little babies."

"I came as soon as I heard," I say. "I drove twenty-four hours."

"You came a long way for nothing," he says. "You wasted your trip."

"Probably," I say.

"Where you been?" he says.

"Away," I say. "I been away."

"No shit?" he says.

"It's been a long time," I say.

"Who are you?" he says.

"I had to get out of here," I say. "I had to leave this place."

"Must be nice," he says. "Did it help?"

"Not so much," I say.

"It never does," he says.

"I was in such a hurry to leave everything behind," I say.

"You never can," he says.

"I brought everything with me," I say.

"You always do," he says, and he starts coughing. He starts coughing, and he can't stop.

I stand and walk into his bathroom. I find a cup on the sink. I turn on the faucet, but nothing comes out.

"Sit down!" he shouts. "Sit your ass down! We ain't got no water! We can't even flush the commodes!"

The sun has gone down. It is dark outside. It is dark inside too. I shine the flashlight along the wall. "I see you got your *Segundo*," I say. "I see you got your submarine."

"What's that?" he says.

"Your pictures," I say. "They must have taken them down before the storm."

"Those ain't mine," he says.

"Pardon me?" I say. I shine the light on the bed.

"Those were his," he says. "That other poor bastard."

"What!" I say. I walk across the room.

"Sit down, goddamnit!" he shouts.

"Shut up," I say. I shine the light on him. He turns his back to me.

"Come here," I say. I grab him by the shoulder.

"Go away!" he screams. "Go away!"

I roll him over. I shine the light on his face. "Who are you?" I say.

"Who am I!" he says. *"Who the hell are you!"*

I let him go. I walk across the room and fall into the chair. "Somebody's son," I say.

"The Navy guy," he says. "The sailor."

"Submariner," I say.

"He's gone, boy," he says. "He was gone before I got here."

"What happened to him?" I say.

"What will happen to me," he says.

I grab the armrests and push myself up.

"You don't have to leave," he says.

"You were right," I say. "I came a long way for nothing."

I move the chair and step into the hallway.

"Don't go!" he says. "I was enjoying the company! We were getting along!"

I walk into him in the darkness. He shines his light on me. "Milam?" he says. "Benjamin Milam?"

I shine my light through the door. "He's in there," I say. "He's been waiting for you."

Someone has left the gate open. I make my way down the stairs. The foyer is dark. The floor is dry. The push brooms are propped up against the front door. "Hello?" I say. I leave the flashlight on the reception desk. "Hello?" I step out under the portico.

There is a full moon shining on the lawn. I hear voices out back, crickets in the azaleas, cicadas in the live oaks. I hear the generators kick in like the rigs on the interstate. I hear the cheering back behind the house.

I walk across the lawn. I right the walkers and the wheelchairs. Too many of these majestic trees were destroyed by the storm. The long, low limbs of the live oaks snapped. The bright white meat of the trunks exposed. I disappear into the Spanish moss.

FIFTY YEARS ago, moving vans disturbed this sleeping town. The trucks arrived first thing in the morning. The movers packed what they could. They loaded all day. The Hoffmans abandoned their stores on the square. The father said goodbye to his fellow businessmen. The little girl said goodbye to her friends at school. The mother sat at the picnic table and stared across the lawn. The movers were hurried, the movers were rushed, and when they left late that night, the tops of their trucks tore the limbs from these trees.

The Baptist church held a service that night. The whole town came. The Hoffmans had left. My mother dressed me in my Sunday school clothes. And when it was over, I didn't walk home. I walked to the big house at the end of the road. There was a bright moon high up in the sky. Someone had hung black sheets on the columns. Someone had hung a black wreath on the door.

I walked up the dark drive. I stepped over broken limbs and

branches. I started off across the yard and tripped over something. I could see the croquet set still standing on the lawn. I could see the white wickets shining in the moonlight.

I walked to the picnic table and selected a mallet. I selected the blue ball, and I began to play. I knew to start at one end of the yard. I knew to hit the ball through the wickets. But this was all I knew. I didn't know if I should head off to the left. I didn't know if I should head off to the right. I decided that it didn't matter. I decided that this was my chance, this was my time to play.

I didn't hear the front door open, I didn't see him step outside, but I did hear someone sobbing, someone weeping under the portico. And then I saw him, and then he saw me, and he started running. I started running too. I didn't even drop the mallet. I just ran. I hurdled the wickets and headed for the trees.

"Hey!" he was shouting. "Hey!" He was chasing after me.

I ran into the live oaks. I hid myself in the moss.

I could see him. He wasn't running. He wasn't shouting. He was walking now across the lawn. I could see him in the moonlight. I could hear him singing, "Come out, come out, wherever you are!" I could see him parting the thick drapes of the Spanish moss. I could hear him whispering, *"Mister Gregory, where are you, Honey?"*

ACKNOWLEDGMENTS

The following stories have been previously published:

"The Bottom" *Reed Magazine*

"Hazard" *Florida Review*

"Old River" *American Short Fiction*

"Open Season" *Southwest Review*

"Return Fire" *The Hopkins Review*

"Shooting Stars" *Night Train*

"Westerns" *Gulf Coast*

"When the Gods Want to Punish You" *Boulevard*

About the Author

GLENN BLAKE has taught at Rice University, the University of Houston, and Johns Hopkins University. A senior editor at *Boulevard* magazine, he is the author of *Drowned Moon* and *Return Fire*. His short stories have appeared in *American Short Fiction*, *Boulevard*, *Southwest Review*, *The Hopkins Review*, *Gulf Coast*, and elsewhere.

Fiction Titles in the Series